Why Stars Burn

The Sirena Diamond Stories

Kathleen Alcalá

Cover art and design by Vincent Sammy

ISBN: 979-8986614694

Rosarium Publishing
P.O. Box 544
Greenbelt, MD 20768-0544

www.rosariumpublishing.com

Table of Contents

This Is Not a Story

This is not a story about a broken heart.This is not a story about what it feels like to be left alone by the person you thought would love you for the rest of your life, or about what it feels like to be deceived.

It might be about what it feels like to deceive yourself, and trying to make the rest of your life conform to that lie. The lie is, "he still loves me."

The truth is, "you are alone."

The reality is, there are more people out there to love, if you will only let yourself go.

This is not a story about heartache. This is not a story about the phone that never rings, the letter that never arrives, or the empty seat next to you at the theatre. This is not a story about bursting into tears when a certain song plays on the radio.

This is a story about putting one foot in front of the other, and finding yourself standing in a place of wonder. The person who brings you this wonder may bring you love as well.

This is not a story.

Cities of Gold

"What do you think you want?" asked Devi.

"A house by the beach. Maybe kids. I don't know."

"Do you want a husband to go with the kids?"

"Oh, I suppose so. Do I have to live with him?"

Devi threw a gum wrapper at her. "That's the general idea. Two kids, a house, a dog. The dad lives with you. You are married and have dinner at your parents' house once a week and the guys watch football."

Sirena tried to imagine this. "Oh, please. What about you? Your family lives all over the world."

"When the time comes, I will consult an astrologer," Devi intoned, dramatically raising her hands, her voice dropping to assume a deep, mysterious tone, "who will find me my prince, the one with whose destiny mine is entwined." She clasped her hands together over her heart.

"You're kidding, right?" Sirena was never quite sure with Devi, since her family was from India.

"Who knows?" said Devi in a normal voice. "It might be as good a way as any to get married. It worked for my parents."

"Yeah, but—that was different. That was in another country and everything."

"How did your parents get together?"

Sirena shrugged. "I don't know. I think my dad went to work for my mom's father. And her dad thought he was okay for her ..."

Devi pointed at her. "See …!"

"But that was different, too!" interrupted Sirena. "That was a long time ago. Things are different now."

"Yeah," said Devi. She didn't sound happy or sad. "Let's go get some lunch. I'm starving."

"Let's pick up some Cokes and go to my grandma's. I haven't seen her recently. She'll feed us."

"Yeah, but I can't eat anything she fixes," said Devi.

Devi was sporadically vegetarian. Sirena had seen her eat lobster before, even though Sirena herself thought it tasted gross.

"Okay, let's pick up drinks and a salad for you and go see my grandma."

Abuela was in her tiny backyard when they pulled up, smoking and throwing scraps of lettuce to her pet duck. In spite of everything people said to her, Abuela would not give up smoking. She was about a million years old. The cement bench on which she sat was surrounded by a riot of herbs and flowers.

Patito squawked loudly upon seeing Sirena and waddled over to her. The pet duck loved Sirena. "This duck is getting big," she cooed to it as the duck nibbled at her hair. "Qué gordito."

"I swear, Sirena," said Devi. "I have never seen anything like this duck. It acts like a dog or something with you."

Sirena exchanged abrazos with her grandmother, and Devi did as well. Then Abuela seated herself carefully on her bench and began to speak in formal cadences to Sirena. Sirena nodded and smiled, sometimes answering "Sí," or shrugging and saying "No sé," as her grandmother spoke. Sirena only understood a little Spanish, and her grandmother spoke no English, but Sirena loved to hear her talk.

Sirena was sure that her grandmother was imparting all of her love and the wisdom of the ages, and if she could only understood her, life would be easier. Sirena knew that her grandmother had lived a hard life, giving birth to children who did not live, including Uncle Mike, who had died in Korea. Somehow, Sirena felt that her grandmother's values were less prosaic, that she understood Sirena's own longings and desperations, her passion, in a way that her parents refused to acknowledge. If they had ever felt passion, for each other or for anything else, Sirena thought, it had long been damped down by the expectations of a middle class life. "What will the neighbors think?" had long superseded "What do I need to feel alive?"

Devi sat on the grass and fed bits of her salad to the duck. It made wonderful contented noises, and Devi giggled and tried to pet it.

Finally, Abuela jumped up and offered them some food. "¡Es hora de comer!" she said.

Abuela always had some cooked beans in a pot on her ancient, dinky stove. She heated lard in a skillet and dipped beans out of the pot, smashing them onto the hot skillet to make refritos. Sirena's stomach grumbled as she walked around the tiny living room, examining the old photos and doilies and miniature paintings from places she would never visit. Her grandmother kept the drapes closed, so that it was cool and dark.

She paused at a photo of her grandparents. She had heard all her life that her grandfather had been either a horrible drunk or a wonderful man. Maybe he had been a wonderful man when he wasn't drunk. They both looked serious in the photo, the man holding his hat, the woman with her carefully marcelled hair. The hairdo was held in place with a diamond clip, and Sirena wondered if her grandmother still had it. She was sure it wasn't made of real diamonds, but she wanted to own it someday.

Six months earlier, she had had a small diamond tattooed on her ankle. Devi had gone with her. It was very tasteful, she thought, a dot design that resembled henna, with lines that radiated from the longer points of the diamonds. The tattoo artist in Venice Beach, Veronika, designed it especially for her.

When Julio saw it, his lip curled up in that way he had.

"It looks …"

"Tacky?" said Sirena at the same time that he said "Cheap."

She knew that he wouldn't like it. That's why she didn't tell him she was going to do it. Still, she didn't expect him to act that bad. Sirena had gotten up and left.

Julio was going to end up just like those other guys from school, marrying the blonde trophy wife who would look good at company receptions. Now he acted like he was better than she was, just because he had gone to law school. She remembered when he couldn't tell which end of a tie was supposed to be on top.

Sirena's grandmother called her to sit at the card table that served as her dining room, placed so that it extended from the kitchen into the living room. Abuela herself refused to sit down, preferring to hover by the stove where she turned tortillas and brought them hot and steaming to Sirena. Abuela ate, holding a plate in one hand, in bits and pieces, like the duck.

Devi came in from the yard, her face flushed. "It's getting hot out there," she said. "Maybe we should go to the beach."

"That sounds nice," said Sirena. "Sit down and eat something. You'll offend grandma if you don't."

Devi sat down and accepted a plain corn tortilla. She sucked at the straw in her drink until she made noises at the bottom. Abuela took her glass of ice and refilled it from the tap.

"Thanks!" said Devi.

"De nada."

"De nada," Devi repeated, then looked uncertainly at Sirena.

"That means, 'you're welcome,'" said Sirena. "Well, really it means, 'it's nothing,' but it means the same thing."

Sirena's grandmother had liked the tattoo right away. "¡Ah, un diamante!' she said.

Sirena's father had changed his name when he went in the Army during World War II. "Otherwise, they would have thought I was Italian," he had said. "This way, everyone can say it and spell it."

But Abuela's name was still Diamante—Anita Diamante. "Como la joya," she would add, like the gem.

Suddenly, there was a commotion outside—brakes squealing and a dog barking.

"¡Patito!" said Abuela. "¿Qué paso con Patito?"

They all ran outside. Sure enough, the duck had gotten out of the yard. It had attracted the attention of one of the many loose mutts in the neighborhood and been chased into the street. Now the duck quacked plaintively, running in frantic circles with traffic stopped in both directions.

Sirena tried to shoo the dog off from where it stood barking and whining, leery of the cars, but attracted by its prey.

Abuela took her apron off over her head and, holding it out in her hands, began to approach Patito, making soothing, clucking noises, oblivious to the cars and their impatient drivers. Just as she was closing in on the duck, a black car came gunning down the curb lane, trying to get around the stalled traffic. The duck noisily became airborne.

"Grandma, no!" screamed Sirena, running back across the street, heedless of her own safety. She saw her grandmother fall. The noisy black car, windows tinted dark, bass notes thumping, ripped by, barely missing Sirena's car parked at the curb as it swerved back into a through lane.

"Grandma!" yelled Sirena. By now, the car nearest to her grandmother had stopped, people were leaning out of their cars to see what was going on, and neighbors watering their lawns were putting down their hoses and coming over. A pack of children materialized out of nowhere.

Devi knelt by Sirena's grandmother.

"Are you okay?" she asked, her voice high.

The old woman looked dazed, but sat up. Dried grass clung to her hair and the side of her face.

"Sí, estoy bien," she said.

"Are you hurt?" asked Sirena. "Are you okay? Did the car hit her?" she said to Devi.

"She jumped out of the way." Devi looked as shook up as Abuela.

Sirena and Devi helped Abuela to her feet. Satisfied that there were no permanent casualties, the drivers got back in their cars and kept driving.

"Can you look for my Grandma's duck?" Sirena asked the children, as much to get rid of them as to find the duck. "If you find it, just tell me where it is. Don't try to catch it, or it will get too scared."

A neighbor handed Devi the balled-up apron, grimy with road grit from the street. The children took off, chattering. Sirena figured they would scare it to death anyway, even if it wasn't already flattened. But she wanted to get her grandmother in the house and make sure she was okay.

They took Abuela into her bedroom and made her lie down. Sirena spread one of the crocheted afghans over her legs, and brought her a glass of water. Soon she was asleep.

Devi had hardly said a word this whole time. She walked into the living room and sat wide-eyed on the green couch with lace doilies on each arm.

"It's my fault," she said.

""What is?" asked Sirena.

"I think I left the gate open when we first came in."

"Don't be silly," said Sirena. "That duck's always getting out. We all forgot about it. She usually puts it in a cage by the side of the house when she's not outside with it."

A little later, there was a shy knock on the front door. Only strangers came to the front door, while everyone else came around through the back garden.

Sirena tried to open the door, which stuck. She tugged harder, and the dim little room was flooded with bright light as the door popped open.

A girl in a red ruffled top and pants stood there chewing on the tip of her ponytail. She was about seven. When she saw Sirena, she turned and looked up to the young man behind her. He looked like he was about twenty. A small boy clung to his pant leg.

"Go ahead, mija, tell her," he said. "About the duck."

Sirena realized he was the father of the children, and had to be a little older.

The girl turned her big eyes back to Sirena, and said, in a husky voice, "We found the duck."

Sirena knelt down on the porch. The girl had tiny gold hoops in her ears. "You did?" She glanced up to the father, who nodded encouragingly. "Is it okay?"

"Yeah," said the girl, "it's in a bathtub."

"Just a second," said Sirena. "I'll be right there." She closed the door without latching it.

"Will you stay with my grandma while I get the duck?" she asked Devi.

"Of course," she said. "Where is it?"

"I don't know," said Sirena. "Close, I hope."

Sirena grabbed a handful of candy from the bowl on the kitchen counter before following the little girl and her father outside. More children waited on the sidewalk. They walked down to the end of the block to cross the busy street. Even at the light, the cars were reluctant to stop for them. She took the little girl's hand, and the man picked up his little boy. Only Sirena and the girl's family crossed.

On the other side, they entered a neighborhood that was a little quieter, with big shade trees. The houses were old, but fixed up. "I can't believe Patito came this far," said Sirena.

"Birds can be pretty smart," said the dad. He seemed as shy as his daughter. Sirena liked that.

They walked almost another block before turning up a driveway. There was a camper truck parked outside the garage.

"I take care of this house when the people are away," explained the father. "They're in Tucson right now."

He unlatched the gate in a chain link fence, and they entered the backyard. It was an oasis of green. Sirena heard a grating noise.

"Is that a frog?" she asked.

"Yup, a big one."

They followed cement stepping stones through big clumps of pampas grass and birds of paradise. Sirena stopped to look at the lettering on one of them. "Freddie Junior," she read out loud. "September 12, 1989."

"Those are their grandkids. There's a step for each one, with their birthdays."

There were a lot of them. The stepping stones led to a small, perfectly oval pond. When Sirena saw the spigot and handles at one end, she realized that it was a bathtub set into the ground. It was surrounded by ferns and flowering plants. "It is a bathtub," she said. The little girl giggled.

Patito was fast asleep on the other side, his head tucked under a wing. He looked like an extra in a movie. One about rajas and sheiks and lonely princesses and lost cities of gold.

"I hate to wake him," said Sirena. "He's had a big day."

"How are you planning to get him back?"

"I don't know," she said. "Maybe if we had a box."

"I can get you one," said the man, and left with his little boy, who had not said a word the whole time Sirena had been with them. The little girl stayed behind with Sirena, still clinging to her hand.

"What's your name?" asked Sirena, sofly. She did not want the duck to wake up and get excited.

"Jasmin," said the girl.

"Jasmin? Like in *Aladdin*?"

The girl nodded. She was staring up at Sirena. "You're pretty," she said.

Sirena smiled. She reached into her pocket and held out a candy in her palm as though offering it to a small animal. The girl hesitated, then took it slowly, letting go of Sirena's hand to unwrap it and pop it into her mouth.

The dad and his little boy returned with a big cardboard box. This time the duck woke up and began pacing uneasily, talking to itself in low quacks.

"Patito ..." said Sirena, soothingly, hoping that her voice would lure the duck. Patito twitched his tail but did not cross the pond to where she stood. The duck eyed the others nervously.

Finally, the father stepped across the pond to where the duck stood between the water and the back fence, grabbing it around the middle before it could react. It quacked and struggled madly. Despite almost losing his balance and dipping his foot into the tub, the man didn't let go.

Sirena held the box open while he put Patito inside. As soon as the top was folded shut, the duck quieted.

"That should do it," the man said. "I can carry it back for you."

"Oh no, thanks," said Sirena. "You've done enough already. And now you're soaked."

The man looked at his squishy tennis shoe and smiled ruefully. Sirena felt a slight surge inside. What would it be like to be married to a man like this, to have a little boy and a daughter named Jasmin?

"My grandma will be really happy to get her duck back. Thanks," she said, "and thank you, Jasmin, for helping."

Sirena carried the cardboard box carefully in front of her. Across the busy street, the jumping children greeted her with shrieks and howls, causing the duck to shift in the dark confines of the box. Sirena handed out the rest of the candy, but refused to open the box and show them the duck.

"It's tired," she said. "It's taking a little nap." She was afraid it would get loose again.

"It's dead, isn't it?" said a little boy.

"No," said Sirena, "listen." She set the box on the hot sidewalk. The children quieted enough to hear the duck shuffling and making small noises in the box.

"It's alive!" they whispered gleefully to each other. "It's alive!"

Sirena carried the box the rest of the way to her grandmother's. At the gate the children waved goodbye, and Sirena carried the box around the side of the house to where her grandmother kept a small mesh-wire pen. It was as much to protect the duck from dogs as to keep it from escaping. She opened the door to the cage and tipped the box on its side.

Patito quacked loudly, ruffling his feathers, but seemed relieved to be in familiar surroundings. Sirena was careful to fasten the wire that held the door shut. "There you go, Patito." She turned on the hose and sprayed some water on the duck, making sure to fill its bowl.

Letting herself in the back door, Sirena felt hot and itchy. "Devi?" she called.

"Here," she answered. Devi was in the kitchen with Sirena's grandmother, drying dishes. Her grandmother had changed into a fresh housedress.

"Míra," said the old woman, lifting her hem like a mischievous schoolgirl to show a long, dark bruise on her leg.

"Ay, Abuela," said Sirena. "¿Quieres ir al doctor?"

"No," her grandmother said, gestering emphatically with her hands. "Estoy bien. No mas tengo magulladura."

"There's a scrape on her arm," said Devi. "But she let me wash it off. I think she's okay." Devi looked better now, relieved.

Sirena looked at the frail skin on her grandmother's arm. This could have been really bad, she thought. "I'm just going to call my dad, okay?" Sirena dialed her parents' number. It was late afternoon by now, and no one answered. She hung up. "They're probably at Costco."

"Míra," said Sirena, imitating her grandmother. She took Abuela's good arm and led her outside. The old woman limped a little. Sirena showed her the duck, quacking to itself in the little pen.

Her grandmother clapped her hands in delight. "¡Ay, qué bueno!" she said. "Se volvio mi Patito, gracias a Dios!"

She said some more things that Sirena didn't understand.

"We've got to go now," said Sirena. She got her purse and keys from inside the house. "Come on, Devi," she said.

"Is your grandmother going to be all right?" asked Devi.

"I think so. She's tough," said Sirena. "I'll have my dad check on her later. He'll want to."

In Sirena's car Devi fiddled with the CD player. "Well, it's too late to go to the beach," she said. "What do you want to do?"

"Don't you have a date later?" asked Sirena. "You always have a date."

"I'm mad at Kevin," she said. "He's two-timing me."

"Like you don't two-time him?" said Sirena, laughing.

"That's different," said Devi. "That's just for fun. This girl really wants him. A friend told me."

"Some friend."

"Let's see a movie," said Devi. "A kung-fu gut buster."

"You like those, don't you?"

"Yeah, I need something loud to get over the excitement at your grandmother's."

Sirena glanced over at Devi. "Look, it's not your fault, okay? She's just fine. Even the duck is fine, although Patito will definitely end up paté someday."

Devi cranked up the CD player, and they joined a long line of cars snaking its way over the Hollywood Hills.

"Let's get one of those magazines," said Sirena, "and look up our horoscopes."

"Forget it," said Devi. "I saw the way you looked at that guy, the one with the little girl. He's taken."

"I know," said Sirena wistfully. She downshifted as traffic slowed, squinting at the road ahead, as though trying to see into the future. "I know."

La Otra

She had never thought of herself as "la otra," the other woman. All she knew was that she had loved him better, and it was only natural that he should leave his fiancé and marry her.

"But that was a long time ago," she would laugh when telling this story to Sirena, who seemed fascinated by her abuela's past. "Back when the animals could talk."

Anita had not been looking for a husband in those days. She already had too many men in her life—four brothers and a widowed father. She cooked and washed from dawn to night, then got up and did it all over again. When the house burned down along with half of the town, it was a relief—there was nothing to wash and nothing to cook. They had no choice but to join up with all the other refugees and walk north.

Some of the men stayed to fight. Her oldest brother, Manuel, stayed with his sweetheart's family to defend what was left of the town. But the soldiers did not want the town. They wanted more soldiers. Both sides. Men and boys were compelled, forced, conscripted, and dragooned, so that brother ended up fighting brother, father fighting son, uncles fighting nephews. It was all mixed up. The crops were deliberately destroyed three years in a row, and finally they had eaten all the seed corn. Better to walk north, where the Americanos were paying good wages.

"Bring extra money and bring extra shoes," was the advise Celso, who led the travelers out of town, gave to them. People brought a lot more than that, but most of it was lost along the way.

Anita claimed not to remember much of the trip. She said she remembered going into towns and begging people for water. She remembered falling asleep while walking, she was so tired. She remembered hiding for hours in the ruins of buildings, all of them trying not to make a sound, while armed men—soldiers or policemen—were around. She remembered a town up north that seemed almost deserted until they found an old woman who showed them a fountain with water. How good it felt to wash her hands and face, her hair, let the water run down the front of her dress. Thirty-eight people started the trek, and thirty-two finished it. Anita remembered that one person died in his sleep, and they found him cold the next morning. She does not remember what happened to the others. Maybe they stayed in some of the towns along the way, or died, or were carried away by a flock of birds.

Sirena watched her grandmother intently when she told these stories, trying to glean from her grandmother's face and hands what she did not understand in words. When Anita got to the part where she described the missing as possibly being carried away to heaven by a flock of birds, the little girl's mouth would go slack with amazement. When she got older, that expression was replaced by a sorrowful smile, the trademark expression of the Diamantes.

By the time they crossed the border, they were all as thin as could be—puro hueso—all bone, Anita would say, holding her fingers a quarter inch apart to show how thin they were. Not like I am now, she would follow, patting her comfortable belly fat.

Sirena would just laugh at her tiny grandmother. Next to her, Sirena felt large and awkward. It was hard to imagine her abuela surviving the long walk, the hunger and thirst, the uncertainty of death waiting for them at every crossroads. But Anita Diamante greeted every dawn with the cautious optimism of a survivor, throwing water on her front steps and sweeping her walkway down to the sidewalk. Let the day bring what it will, she seemed to say—God willing, it will find me here.

As hard as it was to get her grandmother to tell the story of their migration to the United States, it was even harder to get her to tell about how she met her husband and took him away from his intended. She did not tell this story to Sirena until she was older—old enough to know better, old enough to have gained the sorrowful smile.

After all their travails and several false starts, Anita's family went to work picking oranges in Southern California. They settled with other refugees on ground too high and rocky to cultivate, but close enough to meet the foreman at dawn in the orange groves. Anita's father and brothers built a one-room stone house with a cooking shed on the back. Anita asked for one window on the wall facing the street that was a little larger than the small, high windows on the other walls. This had a piece of tin that fitted inside of it to close, fastened by a piece of wire. In summer, Anita took down this shutter and sold aguas frescas to people walking by. Later, she began to sell a few canned goods, and after a year she had a small store where the orange pickers and farmworkers could obtain a few goods near their homes from someone who spoke Spanish. By extending a little credit until payday, "Anita's Tiendita" became popular in the neighborhood.

At first, her father was nervous about Anita being home alone all day with cash in the house, but she assured him that she knew how to handle things. He got her a dog they named Flojo, after the mayor of their town in Mexico. When her father saw how much she was able to make, enough to save, he allowed her to handle all of the finances for the family. Anita was soon the only one who could make change and count to ten in English. On Fridays, she was accompanied to the bank by her three brothers, where the American clerk nervously counted the small bills and wrote out a receipt under their watchful eyes.

With all of this brotherly love and attention, Anita despaired that she would ever marry and start a household of her own.

Whenever her grandmother got to this part, Sirena grew pensive, staring deep into the pattern on the carpet to hide the feelings she knew would show in her eyes.

"Pero ya, mira," her abuela would say, drawing Sirena's attention back to the story. "One day a car drove up and parked across the road. A Model A. A man was driving, and he got out to help a girl from the other side. She was well-dressed, but she acted completely helpless in climbing out of the car."

Here her grandmother would flop her arms like a rag doll. "But once she got on her feet, she grabbed the man's arm like he was the big prize. I could tell that he was embarrassed by her, and I knew then that I would make a better life mate than she!"

Anita would cackle in remembrance at this point, and Sirena would smile in anticipation of the rest of the story.

"It turns out that they had come to our place in the woods to tell us about hygiene. Hygiene! As though, just because we were poor, we didn't know how to take baths. She talked to the women, and he talked to the men. But she was so embarrassed, and used such funny language, that no one knew what she was talking about!"

"You went to the talk?"

"¡Seguro que si! Of course! I had to find out what was going on."

Sirena squirmed in delight. Anita was fully animated now.

"Afterwards, I went up to that man—and I could see that he was handsome, too—and I told him that I could do a better job than that girl.

"He gave me this look—the way you look at something to see if it has more value than it appears to have.

"'You think so?' he said. 'All right then. Here is the address of the next talk. It is right next door here in Corona. And here are some of the brochures that we give people. Take them home and read them, and if you still think you can do a better job, come to the next talk.'

"And so I started going around with him, giving the talks. I was from the people, so I knew how to talk to them in their own language. And then we got married."

Sirena knew there had to be more to the story than that. Like how her father let her go. And what happened to the store, and all her brothers. But she also knew that was all she was going to get out of her grandmother today.

"Bueno," said her grandmother. "Let's go to Pancha's for lunch." Pancha's Comida Mexicana was about two blocks away on a busy commercial street, but they could walk. And her grandmother could order anything she wanted, on the menu or not, and get it. Sirena never turned down a chance to go to Pancha's with her grandmother. Pancha's offered tamales and hope.

The scuffed linoleum floor, a fake brick design, held six small tables and a counter. Sirena's grandmother favored a table by the window, not too far from the kitchen. Settled with sugary hot teas, Sirena ventured another question.

"What was he like?"

"Your abuelo?"

"Yes."

Anita looked outside to the parking lot, as though she could see the Model A on the hot pavement. "Like I said, he was very handsome. You have seen his pictures. But he was handsome enough that people admired him when we passed."

"They weren't admiring you, too?" Sirena teased.

"No, of course not. You see how I am. Maybe they admired me for having him." Anita held up her hand as though she had something important to say.

"But he was also kind. He was very good to me, not like some other men were to their wives." She stirred her tea for a minute. "In those days no one said anything if a man hit his wife. It was his right."

"Some people still think so," said Sirena.

"I know. But it is not right. At least now, women can ask for help, can get protection if they need to. Then, if a woman had children to protect, her parents might take her back, at least for awhile."

"Otherwise?"

Anita looked at her sharply. "Otherwise, she put up with it or had to survive on her own."

Panchita came out from behind the counter to greet her grandmother. "¿Como estas, Anita?"

"Bien, bien gracias. ¿Recuerdas mi nieta, Sirena?"

Sirena nodded and smiled. "Hola," she said.

The older ladies had a ritual they had to go through each time, no matter how many times Sirena had been introduced. They would continue to discuss her as though she was not present.

"¡Ay si, La Sirena! ¡Que guapa esta! ¡Como movie star!"

"Si como no. Y su hermano tambien."

"¿De veras que si? ¿Y donde viva?"

"En otro estado, muy lejos. Ya tiene esposa."

"¿Y Sirena? ¿Ya tiene novio?"

"No, todavia no," said Sirena, jumping into the conversation before her grandmother could say anything.

"Bueno," said Panchita. "No se importa. No te preocupas."

After taking their order Panchita left the table, and Anita could see that Sirena was, nevertheless, distressed.

"Take your time," she said, patting her hand. "You will know when the right one comes along."

"I hope so," said Sirena.

"In the meantime, enjoy being young. Don't let viejas tell you what to do."

Sirena smiled, her first genuine smile all day. "I won't," she said, "except for you."

"Andale," said her grandmother, laughing, as their steaming bowls of menudo arrived. Both stopped talking to eat.

When she had her fill, Sirena's grandmother sat back in her chair, patting her mouth with her paper napkin. "She tried to have me killed, you know."

"Who?"

"La muchacha. La otra."

"The fiancé? The one you took him away from?"

"Yes. But that is another story."

Blue Sunday

It was a blue night, a blue car, and Danny was full of shots of blue tequila.

"Slow down, man. Aren't you going too fast?

"Can't catch me, I'm the gingerbread man."

"Shit, man. I thought I was the crazy one. Just get me back to my old lady in one piece."

"No problem, bro. How's she doing, anyway?"

"Good. She's happy to see me alive."

When Danny came to, he was lying on the ground.

"Get up. I said, get up!"

A foot prodded him.

"Okay, okay," said Danny.

Danny was on his back. He slowly rolled over and got to his hands and knees. Chucho's car was nearby, the passenger door open next to Danny. He vaguely recalled Chucho's nervous laughter as they had careened through the streets of Chino.

"Hijole, man, that cop is mad!" he had said gleefully.

Danny wondered where his cell phone went.

"I said get up!"

"Get up!" the deputy shouted.

"OK," Danny said.

"Get up!" the deputy shouted again.

"I'm going to get up," said Danny, and began to rise.

The deputy fired three shots into Danny.

"Shut the fuck up!" the deputy shouted. "Shut the fuck up!"

Dying had seemed easy in Iraq—people did it every day. And when people were not dying in front of you, your buddies, or the cooks, or the officers, or the civilians who brought in supplies—they were telling you stories about people dying. About how they died, how many, how long it took them, and what it looked like afterwards. Who killed them or who might have killed them.

There was no death with dignity here, only death. Danny spent most of his free time pretending he was someplace else. He plugged his iPod into his head, turned on some tunes, and tried to think about Aimee and the kid they were expecting early next year. Would it be a boy or a girl? It was too soon to tell, but when he went home on leave, they would visit the doctor, and maybe he would do an ultrasound. Danny was ready to think about a little life—a little life after Iraq, if that was possible.

The next thing that woke Danny was sirens. A lot of them.

I ain't dead yet, he thought. A collar was clamped around his neck, and he was rolled onto a stretcher.

"Hustle! Hustle! Hustle!" yelled a woman. I need an IV here, as soon as he's in!"

Some more jostling, then a sharp pain in his arm.

"Go!" yelled another voice.

The ambulance, because he must have been in an ambulance, started up, the siren more muted from inside, and they flew. It reminded him of the cab to the airport in Iraq, but with fewer potholes. He wondered if Chucho was okay.

Next thing Danny knew he was in a bright, noisy room. People kept leaning over him and yelling in his face.

"I'm not deaf, you know," he finally said.

"Oh good, he's conscious," said a male voice. "We thought we were losing you there," he yelled at Danny. "Just keep talking to us."

"Uh, what do you want me to say?"

A bright light was shined in one eye, then the other. "No concussion. Let's give him some fluids," said the man in a normal voice. "Are you in pain?" he said in that voice you use for the deaf, elderly, and foreign born. Danny recognized it as the way he spoke to the Iraqis, as though it would somehow bridge the gap between his English and their understanding.

Danny had to think about this. "Actually, I'm kind of numb on one side."

"Not good," said the doctor. Danny decided to pretend this was a doctor.

"Can you feel this? This?" The doctor pricked him with a pencil tip from his shoulder down his right side.

"It's my arm. I can't feel my arm," said Danny. Damn, he thought. Back from Iraq just in time to die in L.A. The room grew dark again.

Danny could say "stop" and "open" in Arabic. And of course, "Insha Allah"—If God wills it. Sometimes, when he heard the Iraqi men talking and smoking, he could hear them say to each other simply "Insha … insha …" a sort of running refrain, an affirmation of hopes with a strong note of fatalism, if not pessimism.

Danny had gotten used to stepping in front of speeding vehicles. Iraqi drivers seemed to have two speeds—stop, and go flat out, so he, taking their fatalistic attitude, assumed the drivers of speeding trucks would stomp on their brakes before hitting him at the base checkpoint where he was usually stationed as security. If not, his fellow MPs would open fire. It was that simple.

This habit of driving as quickly as possible was soon picked up by the Americans. It started when you got out of air transport and on the road. Because the highway between the airport and the capital was mined, and also without cover, you felt as vulnerable as an ant as soon as you hit the ground. The drivers stepped on it and drove at a suicidal speed, swerving away from any suspicious objects or people, even if it meant directly into the path of oncoming traffic. But the trucks and cars coming the other way were doing the same thing.

Danny became aware of a shooting pain down his left side. It jolted him from sleep, or wherever he had been. Danny remembered the doctor poking him along that side, and feeling nothing. The pain jolted him again. Was this good? Pain was probably better than nothing at all—it meant he was still alive.

"Danny? Danny?" It was his sister Sirena's voice. He felt a cool hand on his right arm, then against his cheek. He opened his eyes, then shut them again quickly against the glare.

"Can you hear me?" she asked. Then a note of her old, mischievous self, his little sister. "Are you in there, Danny?"

He opened his eyes again, caught her silhouette against the window before shutting them again. There was blue sky outside. Good. This meant he was not in Iraq. Where was he, then? He remembered the car chase. The police.

"Chucho … happened to Chucho?"

"My cousin Chucho? He's fine. Don't worry about him. Only you were hurt." Sirena leaned over him.

He could feel her breath on his face, and he tried again to open his eyes, fluttering his eyelids briefly. "What?" he said.

"Do you remember what happened?"

"Yeah. Somebody shot me."

"A sheriff shot you. For nothing. Someone taped it, and it was all over the news."

Danny grunted.

Sirena patted his hand. "Are you thirsty?" Without waiting for a reply, Sirena reached for a glass and placed a straw at his lips.

Danny realized he was in a cervical collar. He opened his lips and sucked.

"Is my neck broken?"

"No. I don't know why you're in that thing. Maybe we can get them to take it off pretty soon."

Sirena looked up at the clock. "Aimee will be here pretty soon, as soon as she drops off the kids."

Soon. Soon. Soon. Her words echoed in his head.

"Soon," he said, and Danny closed his eyes.

At Sarge's urging, Danny tried driving the truck. After grinding the gears around the compound for awhile, he got the hang of it. It was loud and hot inside. It was 100 degrees outside. He had never learned how to drive a stick shift back home. His cousins in L.A., when he emailed them, teased him, told him he was finally a real man.

Danny met Aimee when he was stationed at Barksdale AFB in Louisiana. Her friend was dating another reservist, and the four of them went out one night. The other couple broke up after about two months, but Danny kept seeing Aimee, knowing just that he felt better when he was around her. "This must be love," he thought.

At twenty-five, Danny was one of the last in his family —of his cousins—to marry, except for his little sister. The relatives blamed it on their college educations.

"Gotta get 'em while you're young," said Freddy, a sleeping baby balanced on his thick forearm.

"Gotta get 'em while you still have hair!"

At twenty-nine, working fifty hours a week in a detailing shop, Freddy already looked old to Danny. Danny had gotten his degree in communications and started paying back his debt to Uncle Sam.

Aimee was a Cajun girl, not the sort anyone thought Danny would fall for, with wild red hair and a husky voice. She ordered up a plate of garlic shrimp and a mug of beer for each of them and taught Danny the fine art of peeling shrimp. Then she taught him how to two-step to a zydeco band. It might have been the way she placed her boots on the shrimp shell- and sawdust-covered floor of the nameless crab shack where they danced. It might have been the way she placed her hands on his chest during a slow number and took the wings of his collar between her fingertips before looking up into his eyes. But probably, it was the way she double-clutched her pickup truck without ever glancing at the gear shift that won Danny's heart.

Winning over Aimee's family was another matter. Where Danny came from, the place where they lived would have been called "the tulees." In Louisiana, it was called "the bayou."

Aimee drove her truck south from Shreveport to the end of a paved road, then onto a sandy track that ended in water. Swinging her truck off to one side, they parked next to a stake truck that could have been there five minutes or five years.

"Daddy's home," she said. Wading into the shallows, Aimee retrieved a flat-bottomed boat from the reeds, and they climbed in. They set a bag of groceries and Rikenjaks beer at one end and tucked their coats around it to keep it upright. Then Aimee grabbed the oars and steered them out onto the dark waters. Danny felt like he was in a movie, or at Disneyland, and waited for the giant, audio-animatronic gator to rear up out of the water and snap its plastic jaws at them as they passed by.

"Don't you think they ain't real gators out here," said Aimee, as though reading his mind. "'Cause they is."

Danny kept his hands well within the boat as the sun slipped lower on the horizon.

Danny woke to Aimee's kiss.

"Hey, stranger," she whispered.

"I feel like Sleeping Beauty," he said, "except woken by a princess."

"Were you dreaming?" she asked, pulling her fingers through his short hair.

"Yeah. About you."

"You seem better," she said, pulling her chair closer.

"What about Chucho? Is he hurt?"

"No."

"Oh, that's right."

"They arrested him, but he's out on bail. Your uncle put up the money."

"What's he charged with?"

"Drunk driving. Speeding. Resisting arrest. The works. You were, too, you know."

"I was what?"

"Under arrest. You were chained to the bed. Don't you remember?"

"No. How long have I been here?"

"Five days."

"Am I still chained to the bed?"

"My God, no. Someone taped the whole thing. The sheriff shot you without provocation. Now he's under arrest. Don't you remember anything?"

Danny tried.

"I can get flashes of things, like little snapshots. He told me to get up. I put my hands up, just like he said. But he shot me anyway. He just shot me."

"Well, a couple of lawyers have called. They want us to sue the bastard. They say we have a good case."

"I'm supposed to rejoin my unit in a week."

Aimee threw back her head and laughed. "Soldier, you ain't going nowhere." Then she leaned over and hugged him and burst into tears.

Danny itched even after he'd had the good fortune to shower, which happened at least once a week, the constant dust and grit made him itch. It worked its way under his watchband, under his waistband, under the sweatband of his hat. When he took his boots and socks off, there was a fine mud between his toes that he tried to remove with baby wipes.

Danny wanted to wear a bandana over his face when he worked the checkpoint, but his sergeant said no, it would spook the Iraqi civilians if they could not see his face. When he coughed and spat, his phlegm had grit in it.

A man Danny did not recognize reached up and popped a videotape into the slot in the television bolted to the wall. Grey screen suddenly went to black with white walls, an upswing motion as the camera seemed to be thrust upward, then pointed down.

Danny recognized Chucho's metallic blue Corvette, the front bumper crumpled, white streaks along the side from side-swiping something.

"Get out. Get out!"

A figure on the right was holding a gun with both hands. The door opened, and Danny put his feet on the ground. He didn't see Chucho, although he could hear him yelling.

"It's okay,"said Danny. He had his hands up.

"Get out of the vehicle and down on the ground."

Danny hesitated.

"I said, get down on the ground!" The voice was agitated, angry.

Danny knelt down slowly, then rolled onto the ground.

He remembered now, he had been asleep, or so drunk as to virtually be asleep. That was why he had left his car and ridden with Chucho.

The camera was jostled as the operator tried to focus on the sheriff, on Danny on the ground. He was a light-colored, prone figure on a black background. The quality was poor, bluish for lack of light. It reminded him of night vision goggles.

"Okay, now get up slowly," the voice said. It cracked with tension, near hysteria.

"Okay, I'm getting up now," said Danny. "I'm going to get up."

He rose to his knees, started to put his hands up again.

That was when the shots rang out, five of them. The camera wobbled wildly, but Danny did not see this part because he had shut his eyes and turned away.

"It's okay, darlin'," said Aimee. She clutched his right arm, the good one without all the tubes in it.

Danny could hear Chucho yelling again. He must have still been in the car. Danny opened his eyes and saw himself slumped sideways, close to the open door of the car.

"I told you to lie down!" screamed the sheriff.

Another San Bernardino County sheriff's car pulled up, and Chucho was pulled roughly from the driver's seat.

"He killed my cousin!" Chucho screamed. "He shot him in cold blood!"

"Shut up," said a voice.

Chucho was spread against the far side of the car, searched.

"We are not armed, officer!"

"Just shut up. I'm arresting you on suspicion of drunk driving and eluding an officer." He was led out of camera range as the officer told him his rights.

There was the crackling sound of radios. An ambulance pulled up. The camera seemed to sag with fatigue, again showing Danny prone on the ground.

The ambulance crew hustled out a stretcher, laid it on the ground next to Danny.

"What happened?"

"He tried to attack me."

Danny had a collar clamped around his neck, and he was turned over onto his back.

"Jesus!"

He was placed on the stretcher and taken away. There was a lot of shouting, doors slamming, and the sound of the ambulance siren starting up and fading away.

More radio noise, and a figure slammed the door on the car. The video ended.

The man who put it in had been standing in the corner, watching it silently, observing Danny. "The deputy's name is Troy Ambo," the man announced, "and we are going to sue him into the Stone Age."

"Who are you?" asked Danny.

"I'm your attorney, Jason Ritchie."

Danny glanced at Aimee.

"He called," said Aimee. "He says we don't pay him. He only gets paid if he wins the case."

"Why did he shoot me?" asked Danny.

"That's the million dollar question," said Ritchie. "He claims you lunged at him, that he thought you were armed, but it's pretty clear he was entirely unprovoked.

"Look here." Ritchie pointed a remote at the TV and rewound the tape to where Danny was about to exit the car and place his feet on the ground. He played the tape until Danny started to get up from his prone position.

"Right there," he said, waving the remote and stopping the video where Danny got up to a kneeling position. Ritchie was not a tall man. "He says you reached into your shirt, but you didn't even touch your chest."

Danny tried to look down at his body. Besides the tubes, complicated bandages seemed to cover his chest, and he felt the pull of adhesive tape across the back of his left shoulder. "When can I get this damn collar off?" he asked.

There had been that incident outside of Kirkuk. Two soldiers had died earlier that day, and everyone was jumpy. There was a rumor that a new shipment of weapons had just arrived from Afghanistan, including IEDs.

Danny had spent the previous day escorting a group of Iraqi detainees from one prison to another, always a dangerous business. One man in particular haunted Danny. As he was led out of the foul-smelling holding area along with fifteen others, the man had fixed an eye on Danny, and said in broken English, "I know you. You promised to get me out of here! Where we are going, they will kill me."

Danny did not recognize the man, had never been to that prison before. Did the man have him mixed up with someone else? Was it a ruse?

Danny did not answer, had merely gestured with his rifle for the man to move along onto the truck that would take them to another foul-smelling prison. Danny knew there was torture. Danny knew there was death. On their way to reinforce the battalion that had lost two soldiers, they had stumbled across a trash heap with five more Iraqi bodies, hands fastened with plastic ties behind them, no ID.

Danny did not want to be recognized by anyone in Iraq. He just wanted to do his job and get home.

The following day he was back on the AFB checkpoint. He and Forbes, Yamada and Meyer had been checking IDs and searching cars for five hours. Their shifts had ended an hour before, but their relief had not shown up. They could not leave their posts. All they knew was that there had been an "unexpected delay."

Later, it turned out that Vice President Cheney had made an unannounced visit to the Green Zone to meet with top officials. All members of Danny's squadron who had not been on duty at the time were called in to provide extra security.

"Dang!" said Sgt. Klein when they got back. "They've got hot water twenty-four hours a day in there. And a swimming pool! It's like paradise, while we're roasting out here like hot dogs on a stick!"

The incident had started when a new black Humvee had pulled into line for the checkpoint. The driver got out and walked up to Danny.

"We go around," he said, indicating that they wanted to skip the line.

"All Iraqi citizens must go through the line and show ID," said Danny. Every day, a couple of people tried this stunt.

"He is late for a meeting," said the driver, pointing back at the vehicle. Danny could not see in through the blacked-out windows.

"Sorry," he said, "those are my orders. No exceptions."

The driver went back to the vehicle, and Danny went back to asking for IDs, demanding that car trunks be opened, peering into sweat-smelling interiors at frightened men.

About ten minutes later, the Humvee roared up to him, and the rear window rolled down silently. Danny found himself staring at a man in sunglasses pointing a rifle at him. Danny cocked his own rifle and swallowed hard.

"I mean you no harm," said Danny. He heard the hoarseness in his voice.

"I'll take it from here, soldier," said a voice behind him. Major Samuelson and a translator went up to the Humvee. The translator said something, and the man in sunglasses pulled the muzzle of the gun back into the car without taking his eyes off Danny.

Danny stood down, sweat pouring down his body. Samuelson and the translator got into the Humvee with the armed passenger, and they drove off.

Just then, Danny's relief showed up. "What the hell was that all about?" he asked.

"Oh, man," said Danny. "Not my problem. Not anymore."

"Okay, we're going to try sitting up today."

Danny opened his eyes to see Gladys, the day nurse, rearranging the tubes attached to his body.

He thought of an old joke: "What do you mean 'we,' Kimo Sabe?"

"Very funny," said Gladys. "Okay. Ready?"

"Yeah."

Gladys put one hand behind his back and pushed gently while Danny used his arms to push up. There was some pain and pulling. He caught his breath and grimaced.

"You okay?"

"Not too bad," he said. "Nothing I can't handle."

"Good. The sooner you start moving around, the sooner you can go home. Want to try standing?"

"Sure."

Gladys fitted some slippers on his dangling feet. His legs looked like somebody else's coming out from under the gown.

"You going to give me something to cover my butt?"

"As soon as you stand up, I can put a robe on you," she said.

Danny stood. Muscles pulled. Bones creaked as Gladys held him by the waist.

"How's that?" she asked.

"Good."

"Can you stand by yourself? Here, hold onto the railing." Gladys worked a robe onto Danny's shoulders.

"Well, well! Look who's standing!" It was Danny's father Danny in the doorway.

"Hey," said Danny, pleased in spite of himself.

"He's doing great!" said Gladys. "How about if I get a wheelchair and you can visit in the lounge?"

"What do you think, Danny boy?"

"Good deal." Danny was so pleased that he didn't even object to the eternal nickname.

"Here. Stand right here," Gladys positioned Danny's father next to him, "while I get a wheelchair."

"Have you seen Aimee today?" asked Danny.

"I think so," said Danny. Time had been elastic for him in the hospital. "I think she and Sirena took the kids swimming. Is today Sunday?"

"Yes."

Gladys returned with the wheelchair and Danny's mother. "Look who I found."

"Aye, mijo," said Letty. She made as if to hug Danny, already tearing up.

"Let him sit down first," said Gladys.

Even after two minutes, Danny was grateful for the rest. Gladys attached his bags to a rolling stand and wheeled him down the hall.

"Don't cry, Mom," said Danny.

"I can't help it," she said, dabbing at her eyes. "I'm just so happy to see you can stand, gracias a Dios. It means you're getting better."

Danny's father went straight for the television. "Let's see if the game is on."

"Is that all you can think about?" said his mother. "You come to visit your son, and you want to watch the game?"

"Of course not! It's up to Danny. It's the Final Four!"

"The game is fine, Dad."

Danny's father watched Florida vs. UCLA while his mother recounted what Aimee and the kids had done that day. All were staying with his parents in what had been meant as a short visit upon his return from Iraq. It wasn't a big house, and Danny figured they must all be getting on each other's nerves by now.

"They all got up and had cereal, then went out. So I've just been cleaning all day."

The sound of the game on the television suddenly came up, the announcers rabid with excitement.

"Turn that thing down!" said Danny's mother, turning to her husband angrily.

"I just wanted to hear the scores. I'll turn it back down in a sec."

When Danny spotted Aimee and the kids coming down the hall, he broke into a big grin. Sirena was with them.

"Daddy," said the kids, running up and trying to climb on his lap.

"Careful, careful," said his mother.

Aimee held them back, an arm around each waist. "You can't climb up on Daddy just yet," she said. "Remember, he was hurt. Just give him a kiss."

Danny leaned sideways while each kid, then Aimee, planted a kiss on his cheek. Leaning forward was too hard.

"What's this?" asked Jacob, pointing at the IV feed.

"That's medicine to help Daddy get well," said Aimee.

"And what's this?" he asked, pointing at the urine bag.

"That's how Daddy goes wee wee right now."

The kids giggled. "How?"

"Very carefully," said Danny.

Just then Danny's father turned up the sound again. "Here you are," he said.

A clip from the grainy video taken the night Danny was shot came on.

Danny saw the car window slowly roll down, the stone face of the sheriff. The sheriff's gun was in his hand. He yelled at Danny, who stumbled out of the car, struggling to comply with the man's orders as he barked out commands and expletives. Then he heard himself say it:

"I mean you no harm."

The sheriff ordered him down, then up, and Danny shut his eyes, anticipating the sound of the gun.

"Not in front of the children," Letty hissed.

"Oh, sorry." His father switched the channel to a commercial. Danny's parents continued to argue in low voices in Spanish until Danny's father switched off the TV and stomped out.

"Was that you, Daddy?" asked Jacob.

Danny had turned his wheelchair at the sound of his father's voice. He continued to stare at the blank television, as though the ghostly blue-white images were still on the screen.

"No," he said, "that was somebody else who looks a lot like me, talks a lot like me, but gets shot by the police. That's not me."

"But you were shot. Who shot you?"

Aimee said nothing.

"Somebody," said Danny. "Somebody who thought I was a threat."

He thought about the prisoner in Iraq, the one who said he knew him. Did he know him? It didn't matter. He couldn't help him anymore than he could help himself that Sunday night with Chucho. He wondered if the guy was still alive.

"You know what? I'm gonna get all better pretty soon, and then we're gonna go home. Back to Louisiana."

"Yay!" said Aimee.

"Yay!" said the kids.

"Ay, mijo," said his mother, and started crying again.

"Mom," said Sirena, going over and putting her arm around her mother. "Don't you want him to get better? I'll bet Aimee and the kids are homesick."

"Yes, I want him to get better." She pulled Kleenex from her purse. "I don't know why I'm crying."

"I don't either," said Danny. "It could have been a lot worse."

Illumination

Sirena looked at herself in the mirror. She thought her breasts, all by themselves, made her look unprofessional. She always wore a loose shirt or jacket over a t-shirt to work. This was in part because she was trying to stretch her limited wardrobe of beige and black, but also because she was self-conscious about her large breasts. She had inherited them from her father's mother, Anita Diamante, who carried herself like a queen. Sirena knew she should be proud of her body, like they said in the magazines, but she had known since high school that her breasts made men think of her as just a dumb Mexican. They didn't even hide their comments from her when she passed on the street or at a store, as though she was made of wood and could not hear them. Today, Sirena was already out the door and driving to work before she realized she had forgotten her jacket. Even with a bra built like a battleship too much was, well, too much.

After Sirena arrived her boss came through the door and gave her a long look. About twenty minutes later, the receptionist, Gloria, came into the little room—did it qualify as an office?—where Sirena managed their database and told her that it was Employee Recognition Day and the boss was treating her to lunch. In the six months that Sirena had worked at the real estate office, this was the second time that it had been Employee Recognition Day. It was also the second time that Sirena was singled out to be recognized. Her boss, the owner of the real estate office, was usually in the field or tied up in his office in lengthy negotiations. She seldom saw him except for when he was escorting clients out of his office. Sirena doubted that she was that great of an employee and figured that this would create some resentment on the part of the other fifteen or more people who were constantly in and out of the office. She could hardly say no.

Towson "Just call me Sonny" Rochelle was a sort of caricature of a salesman. He did not seem to realize this, however. He had moved to California from Indiana and still affected the white shoes/white belt look that must have been popular in about 1980. He wore a reddish-brown toupee that he patted constantly and pastel-colored blazers. He had done very well in real estate.

"The Sunshine State has been good to me," he was fond of saying.

Sonny took Sirena to an Olive Garden for lunch. He pulled out a two-for-one coupon and set it out on the table where the waiter would be sure to see it. Sonny told Sirena she could order whatever she wanted. He even encouraged her to order wine, although she didn't drink much. He ordered a martini for himself. Sirena really didn't like the bland pasta dishes they served there, so she tried to order a salad, but Sonny wouldn't let her. It would be, he felt, a waste of the coupon to order a second meal that was so inexpensive. He made her order a dish of scampi on fetuccini as well.

While they waited for their orders, Sonny helped himself to the bread on the table and talked about himself. His eyes seldom rose above her shoulder level. Sirena found herself constructing a barrier of her bread plate, iced tea, and her arms between Sonny's eyes and her breasts. She even took the napkin out of her lap and set it back up in a peak on the table.

"Okay. Let me try this on you."

Here it comes, she thought.

Sonny began lining up the objects in front of him on the table. He appropriated the salt and pepper shakers that Sirena had included in her barrier. She watched the placement of the items—his napkin, his water glass, the shakers—carefully, thinking that he was illustrating a point.

"What if God only exists because we believe in Him?"

Realizing that the objects on the table did not seem to coincide with the question, Sirena shifted her gaze to Sonny's face. "You mean—like a mass hallucination?"

"No, no." He started again, shifting everything slightly to the left. "What if God really existed, okay?" He looked at Sirena in the eyes for the first time that day. "Do you believe in God?"

The question caught her by surprise. "I guess so. Sure, why not?"

"Good. Well, what if the fact that He exists is due solely to the fact that people believe in Him?"

Sirena thought. "So … not a mass hallucination, but a sort of mass projection?"

"Exactly! Very good." Sonny sat back and beamed, as if Sirena were an especially precocious student.

"So that would mean—not that He created us, but that we created Him?"

"Yeah. I think so," he said, suddenly somber. "Jeez, I hadn't thought about it that way. I was still on the first idea."

Sirena continued to follow the thread. "So that would also mean, that if everybody stopped believing in God, He would cease to exist?"

"Not necessarily," said Herb. "In my experience, once you start something, it's a little harder to stop."

Sirena shrugged. "Maybe God was invented by people a long time ago and it doesn't matter, then, what we believe." She was basically saying whatever popped into her head at this point. Sirena wasn't used to having conversations like this with anyone except Devi and people in college late at night. Suddenly, Sirena was conscious of the people around them. The two of them seemed out of place in the restaurant talking about stuff this serious, as though an electrical cloud was forming around them, likely to discharge at any moment.

"Is everything okay here?" asked the waiter.

"Fine, swell," said Sonny. He handed a credit card and the check to him, barely glancing at him.

"Now." He juggled his fork from one hand to the other. "That sounds like dangerous ground we're treading on here."

Sirena nodded.

"We believe in a God, or somebody believes in a God, and so creates Him. Maybe He can continue to exist without our belief, but would He want that? I mean, I wouldn't want that."

Sirena had a flash of an oversized Sonny, plaid pants and pastel jacket, leaning over a celestial desk, not wanting that.

"You're right," she said. "I have a friend who is Hindu, and their gods expect all sorts of things. I don't understand it all, but it's an ongoing relationship."

"Exactly!" said Sonny, punctuating his word with a forefinger. "An ongoing relationship!" He paused when the waiter returned with the credit card receipt, signed it, and stood up. "Shall we go?"

Sirena was glad to. She had run out of philosophical insights along these lines.

"God, you're smart," said Sonny as they walked out to the car. "No offense, but you're so quiet and all."

He didn't say "but you're so brown and all," or "but you're a girl and all," but Sirena knew that's what he really meant.

Back at the office, the positive electronic charge was still evident. When Sonny thanked Sirena for lunch, Gloria rolled her eyes. One of the salesmen muttered something Sirena couldn't hear, but she knew that she would not have liked it. Returning to her tiny room full of printouts and hot computers, the room that doubled as the mail and supply room, Sirena tried to find her way back into the zip codes of Culver City.

After work Sirena stopped at a fast food place. Normally, she tried to skip these unless she was with a friend who demanded fast food, or "fat food," as she called it, but tonight all Sirena wanted, after such a huge lunch, was a shake for dinner. She was anxious to get home. The drive-through line went halfway down the street, so she pulled in the parking lot and walked in. She was almost back to her car, clutching a white paper bag with her chocolate shake in it, when she saw a man stride purposefully out from some bushes between some parked cars, in her direction.

Sirena felt her body tense up. The man wore a bandana low over his forehead, just revealing red-rimmed eyes. He wore dirty black jeans and a black t-shirt. When she saw the knife in his hand, she dropped the white paper sack and stopped. It did not occur to her to scream.

The man stood looking her over. Sirena wanted to fold her arms around her body but was afraid to move. She kept her eyes on him, ready to run. Still, she understood that if she ran, she was prey. Sirena hoped someone would come out to the parking lot.

"What's your name?" he asked, finally.

"Sirena," she answered in a near whisper.

He looked at her with an expression of astonishment on his face. Did she know this man? Had he been a friend of her brother's? Too young, she thought. Or maybe not.

The man fell to one knee in front of her, his head bowed. Sirena did not know what to do. She took a step back. Then he looked up at her, his hand reaching, saying something, when a car with a noisy motor drove by. The man stood, turned, and fled.

Should she go back inside and report it? She'd be stuck there for hours. Sirena looked down and saw the white paper bag leaking brown goo out of one side. The lid must have come off of her shake. It was rapidly melting, leaving a sticky puddle around her shoes. She reached down and picked up the sack. It was then that she noticed the knife.

It was a nasty thing, laying there on the ground, one of those switchblades from Tijuana. Should she pick it up? Sirena couldn't bear to touch it. She kicked it, hard, under a parked car, so at least he would have trouble finding it if he came back. Then Sirena got in her own car and locked the doors and drove home.

In the apartment Sirena locked her door. She took off her sandals and threw them on the floor in the kitchen. They were sticky from the chocolate shake, and she would have to wash the pedals in her car as well. Sirena turned on every light as she passed. She changed into sweats and drank what was left of her shake standing at the kitchen counter, no enjoyment in the act. It was still cold, and Sirena began to shiver.

She got into bed in her sweats, remembering the man's eyes on her, the way he dropped to one knee as though to tie a shoe, or worship her. What was that all about, anyway? What was it he had said? It sounded like "I have inquired about illumination."

Another cheeseburger in paradise, she thought.

Sirena cleaned up the mess from her shake and dialed Devi's number.

"Yes?"

Devi never said "hello," but always "Yes?" in a tone not quite cool, and not quite friendly. Something from her parents, no doubt.

"Yes?"

"Hi. It's me."

"Oh, yes? Another mad day at the office?"

"Hey, I was recognized as an outstanding employee."

"Congratulations. Weren't you just recognized?"

"In September. And the boss took me out to lunch again."

"Where did you go?"

"The Olive Garden. With a coupon."

"Oh, my. How special."

"We had this conversation. About God."

"Very deep?"

"Very. What if God is a projection of human belief. Real, but a projection."

"What if God, or the gods, are a projection. Then they would be our children, wouldn't they? Rather than we theirs."

"Is that bad?"

"Not so bad. Maybe we would have to grow up a little, behave like adults, if we knew that."

"Then something strange happened after work. Pretty creepy."

"What?"

"I stopped at Sno-Freeze for a shake for dinner, since Sonny forced me to have a giant lunch. A guy pulled a knife on me in the parking lot."

"Sirena! Are you okay?"

"I'm fine. He dropped it. He got down on his knees, then kind of looked at me. Then he got up and ran away."

"That's all?"

"He didn't … do anything. It was right in the middle of the parking lot with people all around."

"Did someone see you?"

"I don't know. It all happened so fast."

"Sirena, girl, you have got to be more careful. Look around before you get out of your car."

"It was when I came out of Sno-Freeze. He just—appeared."

"Maybe you projected him."

"Like God? That's a depressing thought. My god is a psycho in a red bandana. He said something strange, I think."

"What?"

"I'm not exactly sure. It sounded like, 'I have inquired about illumination.'"

"He said this before or after he dropped the knife?"

"After."

"Hmmm. Maybe you were his projection."

"Oh, stop it."

"I mean it. Maybe he meant to drag you off into the bushes, but then he realized that you were his goddess."

"That's so weird, Devi."

"No weirder than what happened. It's only an interpretation."

"What about Sonny?"

"Your boss? What about him? Don't you want to be employee of the month permanently?"

"Not especially. I just want to do my job."

"You need to set your sights higher. Maybe look for another position."

"Maybe. Do they need a database manager at your firm?"

"No, but they might need a goddess."

"Devi."

"I'm sorry. I'm so glad you weren't hurt."

"Yeah. Me, too."

"I'll call you tomorrow, and maybe we can catch a movie."

"Good."

Sirena dreamed that night of Hindu gods like the ones in the posters in Devi's kitchen. They seemed to have a cruel streak, even with their benign smiles.

In the dream the gods and goddesses, some blue-skinned, others multi-armed, bare-breasted, seemed to be singing and dancing. What was that word Devi used? Bollywood, from the film industry in Bombay. Yes, Sirena seemed to be watching a Bollywood production of the gods. During all of this, she was trying to pick up her chocolate shake, even scraping up a part of it that had spilled on the ground like dark blood.

In the morning she tried to remember what the gods had been singing, so she could tell Devi, ask what it meant. But all she could remember, over her first cup of coffee, was the way their mouths and eyes moved, like separate beings from the gods themselves.

Every Love Story is Different

Or is it that every love story is the same? Sirena could never remember. She only knew that every love story was supposed to have a happy ending, but seldom did.

Sirena was cooking dinner when she heard a knock at the door. Normally, she wouldn't answer at this hour, but she had seen the UPS truck drive up and drive away, and she had been expecting a package. She had placed her order two weeks ago, and it was supposed to be shipped the next day. They just don't say how long it takes to arrive.

The man at the door wasn't from UPS, but Sirena thought she had seen him before.

"Good afternoon," he said. "I think this is for you. I live downstairs."

He handed her a package with her name, but his apartment number.

"Thanks," she said. "I've been expecting this."

"You're welcome," he said, then hesitated. "My name is Jim. Jim Peterson." He stuck out his hand.

Sirena shifted the package awkwardly to take his hand. "Thank you. I appreciate it." Since her name was on the package, she didn't bother to say it again.

Sirena smiled and retreated back into her apartment. She was afraid to get too friendly with the neighbors. People were always trying to fix her up with men, and men were always trying to get fixed up with her. Although her long-distance relationship with Julio was crumbling, the last thing she wanted was another complication. All she really felt like doing, when she wasn't busy with work, was to stay home and cry.

Sirena took the rice off the stove and set it aside to continue steaming. Using a kitchen knife, she opened the package with that slight surge of anticipation, only to find a note that said, "The size or color you requested is out of stock, but we have substituted an item we hope will suffice." Inside were pale brown shoes, not the dark red she had ordered. They had sent "Palomino" instead of "Paprika."

Sirena tried on one shoe in a desultory fashion. She had already planned the outfits the other shoes would have gone with. She had harbored a vague idea that she would wear them out to a nice dinner the next time she saw Julio. While these fit, the color was too boring to believe. She sighed and put the shoe back in the box, closed it, and went into the kitchen to eat something. Couldn't anything go right for her?

The next morning, while getting ready for work, Sirena tried on the shoes again. They would go with her beige suit. She had a couple of those "weekender" outfits in which all the pieces match, one set in beige and one in black, and she wore one piece or another almost every day to work. It was a cheap way to look put together, although she knew, when she went out on her lunch hour, that the outfits screamed "I work in an office, and I don't get paid much!" to everyone on the street. She decided to wear the new shoes to work that day.

Sirena worked in a real estate office. She mailed circulars to whole zip codes at a time, updating the data bases constantly, printing out labels, and putting them on envelopes. It wasn't very interesting, but the people were nice to her. They were encouraging her to study for a real estate license, and she was thinking about it. Or at least, pretending to think about it.

"After all, you can always sell real estate, no matter what else you decide to do," said the office manager. "It's a good part-time job after you're married and have kids."

Even the word marriage made Sirena's eyes well up. She didn't want to hear about it.

Julio was a lawyer, sort of. He had finished law school but had not passed the bar exam during his first try. He was studying to take it again. In the meantime, he was working for a congressman in Washington, D.C.

"Come with me," he had said.

"But I have a job," said Sirena.

"You can get one there. There are lots of jobs, and they pay better, too."

Sirena was not sure. Her whole family was in California. Her father fixed her car for her, and she knew her parents would have kittens if she moved to Washington just to be with Julio, even if they had separate apartments.

"You're just there for awhile, right? I thought you were planning to come back and take the bar, set up practice in California."

"Of course, I will, but I miss you. Why won't you do this for me?"

Sirena wasn't sure. She disliked the idea of picking up and moving across the country. It had been hard enough to find this apartment. She didn't think her car would make the three thousand-mile trip. "I'll think about it," she said.

But every time she thought about it, Sirena came up with more reasons not to move. It was cold there. It was unsafe. It was expensive. If she decided to go back to school, she would certainly go to a college in California, might even take some classes part-time.

Soon the rumor mills were buzzing with Julio's exploits in Washington. He went to a reception with somebody. He was seen at a restaurant with somebody else. They had both attended Cal State Fullerton, so there was no shortage of people to tell Sirena what was going on. When you are dating someone, the whole country is a small town, Sirena discovered.

"You can't expect me to stay home by myself," said Julio on the phone. He sounded defensive. "Besides, it's part of the job. That's how you do business here, you talk to people at these receptions."

Sirena didn't say the things she wanted to say. She figured she deserved it for not being the faithful girlfriend, the follow-your-guy-anywhere type everyone seemed to expect. Instead, she admired her friend Devi.

Devi's parents were from India, but she was a very modern girl. Devi worked down the street from Sirena's office, where she was a draftsman for an architectural firm, and sometimes they met for lunch. Devi's exploits left Sirena laughing and gasping at her audacity. Once, while entertaining a boyfriend in bed, another came to the door. Throwing on a robe, Devi answered the door with all the imperiousness she could muster, drawing herself up to her full 5′2″.

"Don't you ever, ever again come to my place without calling first," she had said. "Can't you see that I am not well?" The boyfriend at the door retreated with hasty apologies, and Devi was able to salvage both relationships.

Instead, Sirena bought shoes. She even had a pair of Manolo Blahniks, although she didn't know where she would ever wear them. They had heels that looked like bananas.

About a week later, Jim held the door for her as she came into the apartment building with a bag of groceries.

"After you, ma'am," he said. There was something cowboyish about him, of the old-fashioned gentleman.

"Thanks," said Sirena.

"Do you like to fly?"

"Fly? As in get in an airplane and fly?" Sirena shrugged. "Not particularly. It's too crowded."

"How about in a private plane? I have a pilot's license, and sometimes I rent a plane and go places for the day, like Palm Springs or Santa Barbara."

"That sounds really nice," said Sirena.

"How about next weekend?" he asked.

"Oh, no, that's my birthday," she said. It came out before she could stop it.

"All the better! We could go someplace special."

"Oh, thanks, but I don't think so." Sirena was trying to think. "I'm sure my parents are expecting me home. My mother likes to make a big dinner."

"Well, I could fly you there."

Sirena gave him a skeptical look. "It's not that far. But thanks." She walked away, hoping that would end the conversation.

"Maybe some other time," Jim called after her.

Sirena put her groceries away. Then she went in the bedroom and put on the Manolo Blahniks and admired them in the mirror. They made her think of Beverly Hills and women with too-tan skin and nothing better to do than shop. She thought of herself stepping out of a private plane in them in Palm Springs. She saw herself falling down on the tarmac and spraining her ankle. She shook her head and slipped out of the shoes. Jim was kind of cute, but she thought he was too old. If he could fly a plane, he was probably military or something, not her type.

"I can't get away this weekend," said Julio, who went by Mike now, his middle name. "Too much work. I'm sorry, baby. But I still love you."

Sirena hung up the phone. He had waited until Thursday night to tell her. She imagined dinner with her parents. They would ask her about work during dinner, be nice to her, then her father would retreat to the den and put the television on full blast while her mother bad-mouthed Julio for not caring enough to come and see Sirena for her birthday. Sirena's parents had hated all of her boyfriends, starting in high school, yet they were dying for her to get married. She couldn't figure out how they expected her to do that without dating.

They wanted what her brother Danny called "the immaculate marriage." It had been easy for him. He came home from college one day and announced that he was engaged, and everybody was happy. His wife, Connie, was nice, and their mother only complained when Danny and Connie moved to the Midwest for his job. She couldn't blame that on his wife.

Sirena decided to call her parents and say she was going out with a friend, then stay home by herself and wallow in misery, watch late-night TV and eat popcorn. There's a plan! she thought.

The next day Sirena told Devi about the man in her apartment building.

"You should go!" Devi urged. "Even if you don't like him, you'll never meet anyone if you don't get out."

"I don't want to meet anyone," said Sirena. "I want Julio to come home."

"Home is where you make it, girl," said Devi. "And it sounds like he has made his home elsewhere."

This is not what Sirena wanted to hear.

‡‡‡

Saturday morning Sirena decided to pretend like it was just another day. Maybe Julio would at least call. She threw on some old clothes and went downstairs to do a load of laundry. She got an early start because she was wary of leaving her clothes in the laundry room later in the day when there was more traffic. Someone had once taken a set of lace panties and a matching camisole, the most expensive underwear she had.

Coming back upstairs, she bumped into Jim. "Oh, hi," she said, embarrassed. Her hair was dirty. She hadn't even taken a shower yet.

"Sirena!" he said. "You're still here!"

"Yeah," she said. "It only takes an hour to get to my parents'."

"There's still time," he said. I could take you to Catalina Island and back in time to have dinner with your folks. In fact, I just checked the weather. It's perfect!"

"Oh, thanks," said Sirena. "That's sweet. But I'm busy. I have a lot of things to do this morning." She slunk off down the hall.

Sirena took a shower and went downstairs to get her stuff out of the dryer, her hair still wet. By now, all the washers were rotating at full tilt. In an hour all the dryers would be going. Sirena almost never saw people down here, but the machines in the laundry room were almost continually in use. It was a mystery to her.

Lugging the laundry basket up the one flight of stairs to the main floor then to the elevator, she wandered down her hall and returned to her apartment. She looked forward to a Saturday by herself. She tried not to glance at the phone, which seemed even quieter than usual. Maybe she would go out to lunch and see a movie.

There was a knock at the door. Sirena had a feeling who it was.

"Listen," said Jim. "I don't want you to think I'm too forward, but I checked at the airport, and there's a plane available. We can be there in fifteen minutes, and I can get you to Catalina and back in five, maybe six hours. It's a perfect day. What do you say?"

Sirena just looked at him. "You know, I don't even know you," she said. His attentions hurt all the more because of the silent phone. She felt a pain, an actual pain, in her heart.

Then the phone rang.

"Just a minute!" she yelled in the direction of the phone, and slammed the door in Jim's face. When she picked up the receiver, there was only a dial tone. Sirena burst into tears.

After a few minutes, Jim knocked again. Sirena ignored it.

"Sirena," he called.

She got up and opened the door, then threw herself back on the couch. "Can't you see I'm a wreck?" she said. "Just fly. Go have a good time."

"Sirena," said Jim, taking a step into the apartment, "I know it's none of my business, but you'll have a better time with me. You don't even have to talk to me. Just enjoy the ride."

Sirena kept crying, but he didn't leave. He just stood there. "Okay, fine," she said, finally. "But I have to change."

"That's great!" said Jim. "I'll call and reserve the plane, make sure it's fueled up. I'll meet you back here in twenty minutes?"

Sirena nodded.

It was just a few minutes to the Burbank airport. Jim had a small but nicely kept car. There was an official-looking decal on the back.

"Are you in the Navy?" asked Sirena. She felt awful, but she figured she should at least try to be pleasant. Her eyes felt like pinholes behind her dark glasses.

"Used to be," he said. "Now I'm a civilian who works for the Navy."

"Doing what?"

Jim described something Sirena didn't really listen to, something about tracking inventory.

They drove to the far end of the airport where the private planes were kept. Jim said hi to all the people as though he knew them. They looked at her curiously, and she could tell that he was proud to show her off, introducing her with his hand sort of hovering above her back like she was a prize at the county fair. Sirena hated that. Jim filled out some paperwork before someone handed him a set of keys, just like for a car.

They walked out on the tarmac to a little plane. Jim walked around it, naming and describing it, a Cessna something-or-other. When they climbed in, she put on a seatbelt while Jim described how all the controls worked.

"Just in case I have a heart attack and you have to take over the controls." Sirena could not tell if he was kidding or not, but she tried to pay attention. After following a safety checklist, they took off.

The ascent was very steep, steeper than in a commercial jet. Sirena found herself gripping the sides of the seat.

"Are you okay?" asked Jim.

"I'm fine," she said. "It's fun."

"Good. Wait until you see the view from up here."

Soon they could see the ocean. It was a brilliant turquoise blue with the white beaches running along beneath them, tiny cars moving up and down the coast highway.

"We are going to fly west, then south to get to Catalina," said Jim. "There's a big no-fly zone around LAX, which is just as well."

After a few minutes the land was behind them, and the ocean stretched before them in a bright, glimmering sheet. Sirena was glad she was wearing sunglasses.

Jim talked and talked about himself. He was going on about his pension plan. Apparently, the military had really good benefits, even for its civilian employees. Sirena drifted, imagined herself as a bird, an albatross that can sleep while it is flying.

Sirena dreamed that she could see everything, all the way across the country. She dreamed that she could see Julio sitting at an outdoor café in Washington. With a girl, naturally. Sirena tried to zoom in closer and get a look at her. She could tell that Julio was lying to her, saying things about himself that weren't true. He was wearing a suit and tie and kept pulling at his collar as though he was uncomfortable. You should be, thought Sirena.

When the plane began to descend, Sirena woke up. She looked over at Jim, who smiled broadly.

"Have a good nap?"

"Yes. Sorry, I didn't mean to fall asleep."

"It's fine with me. That shows how comfortable you are with my flying."

Sirena was embarrassed to have fallen asleep in front of this man she hardly knew. She didn't like the idea of him watching her sleep. She looked at her watch, but only twenty minutes had passed. She felt light-headed.

"There's Catalina Island," said Jim, pointing to the south. "We'll swing around and approach from the east."

It was very green and rose steeply out of the water. There was a ship in the bay. It looked like something out of a movie—a Muppet movie.

Again, the descent was steep, and they landed at a tiny airport. It had been blasted out of the tops of two mountains, and the rubble used to level the valley between them. "You probably couldn't do that now," said Jim. "Some environmentalist would object."

They took a shuttle bus ten miles into Avalon, where they walked up Crescent Avenue. Jim talked about this restaurant he loved, one he used to visit with his ex-wife. The street was crowded with tourists and curio shops and places selling salt water taffy. At the harbor they stopped and watched as children and teens dove for coins that people threw over the sides of boats. Sirena shivered when she saw them. They looked inhuman, mer-like, as they wriggled in the dark green waters. They opened their mouths like fish and took the coins between their teeth. Sirena saw a girl surface, slick back her hair, and climb out. When she opened her mouth, shining silver fell out into her cupped hands.

After walking up and down the street a couple of times, Jim decided on a café. He wasn't sure if it was the same one he was looking for.

"It's been awhile," he admitted.

They ate a late lunch outdoors. "How do all these people get here?" asked Sirena.

"They come over by boat, the Catalina Express from Long Beach, or a few by plane. Some people actually live here, though mostly in the summer."

Sirena tried to imagine living on an island. It seemed very romantic, but also boring. Confining. What if you had a fight with someone?

Behind her, a large man shifted his chair uneasily on the deck. "I'll bet you do," he mumbled.

"What's that?" said the woman across from him.

"I said, 'I'll bet you do!'"

Sirena and Jim exchanged looks.

"Now that's just the sort of thing I would expect you to say," answered the woman.

The man set his glass down with a clunk. Sirena pulled her chair a little closer to the table. Jim pulled the table toward himself to give her more room.

"Now see here," said the man. "I have just as much right to my opinion as you do!"

"More," said the woman.

"More," repeated the man, drawing out the word. "Now what's that supposed to mean?"

"It means that you think you have more of a right to your opinion than I do."

"I said no such thing. Stop putting words in my mouth. I said no such thing!" His chair scraped and rumbled on the deck.

Sirena felt the back of her neck tense up, as though preparing for blows from behind.

"I don't need to," the woman continued.

"What the hell's the matter with you?" he asked.

"What the hell's the matter with you?"

A waiter suddenly appeared at the couple's table. "Will there be anything else?" he asked.

"Just the goddam check," said the man. "How soon does that boat leave?"

The air seemed lighter, somehow, clearer, after the couple left.

Jim lifted his glass of beer and held it out. "Happy birthday," he said.

"Thanks," said Sirena. He continued to hold his beer aloft until she picked up her iced tea and touched glasses with him.

"You're about ... twenty-five, right?" he said, squinting at her in the strong light. "Although you don't have to tell me if you don't want to," he added.

"Twenty-three," she said, quietly.

"Wow," he said. "You're even younger than I thought."

Sirena didn't say anything.

"So tell me why you're so unhappy with your boyfriend."

Sirena shrugged. "Is it that obvious?"

"Sure," said Jim. "I was married once, for a little while."

"Then I don't need to explain," said Sirena. "Every love story is the same."

"I sure hope not," said Jim. "Go on, it will make you feel better."

Sirena's eyes welled up. "No, it won't."

They sat in silence while Sirena took small sips of her iced tea and tried to compose herself. She really should try to be nice, she thought. She tried to think of something to say.

"Thank you for doing this," she said. "I wish I were better company."

"It's a pleasure," said Jim, raising his glass to her again. "I just hate to see a lady cry, though, especially on her birthday. What can I do to cheer you up?"

Be Julio, she thought, but forced a smile.

On the flight back, they could begin to see the eastern horizon darkening behind the mountains, a darker blue rim on the iris of the earth. They could see a brown cloud seeping north from the L.A. basin into the outlying suburbs.

"What a lot of smog," said Sirena.

"Yup, it's pretty bad."

When they finally landed at the airport, Jim made some more small talk with the staff. Then he took her home. As they walked into the apartment building, it was as though nothing at all had changed, as though Sirena had not gone anywhere.

They stood awkwardly at her door.

"Thank you," she said again. "That was really nice. But I have to get ready to go to my parents'."

"What are you doing next weekend?" asked Jim.

"I don't know," said Sirena, looking at the floor. "I really don't."

"Can I call you?"

"I don't know," said Sirena, then, more firmly, "Look. I have to go now."

"I understand," said Jim, and walked away. "See you soon."

Sirena entered her apartment and closed the door with relief. There was a message on her answering machine, two messages. One from her parents, one from Julio. Both of them wanted to know where she was.

Sirena went into the bedroom and took off the brown shoes. She carried them into the kitchen and tried to wash off the soles with a damp paper towel. After some scrutiny she decided that it would be difficult to tell she had worn them. She had been careful not to scuff them up, not to drag her feet. Then she put them back in the box and filled out the return form. Under reason for return she checked "wrong color." Sirena decided to hold out for the red ones after all, or get her money back.

Sirena put on her Manolo Blahniks and tottered around in front of the mirror. You look good, she thought. Her eyes weren't even swollen anymore from crying earlier in the day. She wanted to call Devi, tell her about Jim, but remembered that she was out of town.

Then she went out. Driving down Alameda Avenue, Sirena realized that she needed to stay out for a couple of hours; long enough for Jim to think she was gone, long enough to pretend she had some place to go.

When she returned early the next day, there were roses on the floor outside her door.

Why Stars Burn

Instead of going to her parents' house on her birthday, Sirena went to a movie. She went to a lot of movies at once, a festival of animated shorts, in Venice Beach. It was cool, it was dark, and a great place to avoid everyone—her parents, her friends, her telephone that rang but did not tell her what she wanted to hear.

Settled down in a good seat, a huge box of popcorn next to her, Sirena laughed and gasped her way through the antics of the characters on the screen. She longed for friends as true and lovers as sexy as those on the screen. She shuddered at the possibilities of war, of being thrown in jail for a crime she didn't commit, of meeting a suave Frenchman in an elevator to the moon.

At the break, standing in the lobby, Sirena started talking to someone about her own age who had been sitting near her. He was tallish with the type of square cheekbones you would see on a Swede, but dark. He did a wonderful imitation of one of the characters hanging from the edge of a wall, a dragon above him, a rushing river below, before letting go with one hand, holding his nose, and jumping in, only to be caught by a giant bird and whisked off to a new adventure.

"My name is Bullitt—two *l*s, two *t*s," he finally said.

"Bullitt?" asked Sirena. She didn't know if he was still kidding. "Is that your first name or your last?"

"My first. I'm not sure what my parents were thinking."

"Bullitt," Sirena repeated. "Kind of like 'the man of steel.'"

"Maybe that's it. They hoped I would be indestructible."

When the festival started up again, they went into the theater talking together, and he took the seat beside her. Sirena laughed twice as hard as she had laughed before and giggled a lot in between. Even though they could barely see each other, Sirena and Bullitt exchanged glances in the dark at especially droll moments.

It was over shortly before midnight, and they emerged into the cool, damp air with relief.

"Phew," said Sirena. "It got hot in there." She pushed her hair back from her face.

"Probably because we were laughing so hard," said Bullitt.

"Yeah, probably." They lingered in front of the theatre as others made their way past them. Sirena did not want to return to her own apartment, the blinking light on the message machine. Or no light at all.

"Would you like to get a cup of coffee?" she asked Bullitt.

"At this hour?"

"Well, you know. Or something. How about pie?"

"Pie sounds great."

They took both cars and drove to a Denny's. Not a lot of places were open at that hour. Bullitt had rum raisin. Sirena ate key lime pie without whipped cream. On top of the popcorn, Sirena knew she would probably have indigestion the next day.

"Stay with me a little longer," said Sirena, after they piled their change on the table to pay.

"We'll have to eat more pie."

"Not here. Get your car and follow me."

Sirena led Bullitt to Santa Monica, where her friend Devi lived.

"Wow. This is cool," said Bulllit, looking at the posters on the walls. "Have you traveled to all these places?"

"This is my friend's place," said Sirena. "Her family is from India. She's out of town, and I'm keeping an eye on it for her. She won't mind."

Sirena put her arms around Bullitt's neck and kissed him. When she took off his shirt, she could feel ridges on his back. She pulled back to look at him.

"What happened?" she asked, tracing the radiating lines from the right side of his spine at the base of his rib cage.

"That's the real reason I'm named Bullitt," he said, sleepily, and lay down on his stomach. "Don't stop, that feels good. When my mom was pregnant, she was shot during a robbery. I was delivered early. But I was okay, just a big scar."

Sirena didn't know what do say. "What about your mom?"

"She got well. She was nervous about going out for a long time, but she got over it."

"Are you an only child?"

"Yeah. I was her first and only. The bullet might have messed her up a little to have more children."

"Right." Sirena drew loops and arrows across his back with her nails. "You were lucky."

"Yup, always have been."

"It looks like a star—like a shooting star burned through the atmosphere and landed on you, branding you forever as a star child."

"Mmm. Tell me more."

"All over the universe are other star children. Someday you will receive a call. No one knows where or when, but it will be your duty, the duty of all star children, to answer the call and save the universe." Sirena felt herself using Devi's inflections to make the story more dramatic.

"I was afraid of that."

"Of what?"

"That this would entail saving the universe."

"What could be more important?"

"Well, things that I have more control over. Like getting to work on time. Or paying my bills."

"Are those things under control?"

"More or less."

"Then there you go. You've got the small stuff down, later you will move on to the big stuff."

Sirena took off her own clothes and snuggled under the blankets. Bullitt told her she was beautiful. Sirena had only been with her boyfriend before, but she didn't tell that to Bullitt. He had very dark hair against light skin. She touched the places where it came to a point—at his sideburns, at the nape of his neck, in a dark "v" at the base of his spine. When he held himself over her, Sirena could feel the scar under her left hand, like a pattern placed there just for holding on to. She found her fingers returning to it again and again, as though the scar were a sort of braille that would explain the mystery of this life to her.

"Tell me more about the star children," Bullitt said later.

"I think that's what really happened to you," said Sirena, keeping her eyes closed. She was folded around a pillow. "Your parents made up the part about the robbery because it was easier to explain to people than what really happened.

"They were outside, maybe camping in the mountains, watching a meteor shower. Something fell near where they were sitting, out in the trees. They went to look. It was burning hot. Stars burn. Your father put it in a box so that it wouldn't start a forest fire, but it was too heavy to lift. So your mother tried to help. And the star slipped out and went into her side, where it lodged in your back."

There was silence as they contemplated this possibility, his parents struggling to lift the heavy box from the pine needle-covered ground, his mother round with pregnancy, an edge of the box slipping so that the star slipped out.

"That would explain a lot," said Bullitt.

Sirena hesitated. "Was there a bullet in you when you were born?" she asked.

"Actually, no. It must have just passed through her. They did an emergency C-section to deliver me. They never found it. It was kind of strange."

"See? It was a star!"

"Maybe so. Tell me about the other star children."

"They are all over the universe, each with a scar like your own. They are all about your age. What is your age?"

"Twenty-three."

Then Sirena remembered. "Today is my birthday." She glanced over at Devi's clock. "Yesterday was my birthday."

Bullitt sat up on one elbow. "Really! Happy birthday!" Then, "Why weren't you out with your friends? It was even a Saturday."

Sirena sighed. "I don't know. I didn't really feel like it. I was supposed to drive to my parents' house, but I just … I don't know." Sirena was trying not to cry.

"Don't worry about it," said Bullitt, pulling her close. "I'm glad you chose to spend it with me. Now," he said, "tell me more about the star children."

"When the time comes," said Sirena, brushing the tears from her eyes, "you will be gathered together to fight the forces of evil." Her face struggled with a smile. "You will wear very attractive uniforms and dark glasses." Her voice cracked as she laughed and cried at the same time.

"This is starting to sound familiar. I don't have to wear a long trenchcoat, do I?"

"Okay, well, maybe not the dark glasses." She swallowed and tried to control her voice. "But definitely the attractive uniform that shows off your perfect physique. And you will discover that you have special powers that you have not even dreamed of."

"Like what?"

"Umm, special universe-saving powers. Like the ability to teleport across time and space. Come on, help me out here. What kind of powers would star children have?"

"The ability to hear colors. To speak every language ever spoken, so they can talk to each other."

"That's good. I'd like to be able to do that. My grandma speaks only Spanish. I can sort of understand her, but I can't say a lot of things to her that I would like to."

"Like what?"

"Like how much I love her and that I want her to be careful and take care of herself."

"Does she live here?"

"Yeah, I see her most weekends. She still lives alone, cooks for herself and everything. But she lives on a busy street, and it's hard, sometimes, for her to get to the store and stuff."

"How about your parents? Do they take care of her?"

"Yeah." Sirena rolled onto her back and stared at the ceiling. "My Dad stops by sometimes. She and my mom don't get along. And my grandma just likes to do things for herself. She's always been like that."

As they talked, the night grew as dark as it gets in Santa Monica, and the traffic noise gradually died down to the occasional noisy muffler.

After a long while, Bullitt said, "You know what the star children are most afraid of?" He was whispering into the top of her head.

"What?" asked Sirena.

"Loneliness. Since they're scattered on different planets across the universe, each is afraid he or she is the only one, the only star child."

"But don't they know? Don't they know they have a special mission?" Sirena tried to keep her tone light.

"I didn't know. Until tonight, when you told me."

Bullitt turned her face up to his and kissed her. He seemed to want to burrow into her, blindly. Later, Sirena lay and listened as the night became even more still, approaching that moment before the day renews itself. She listened hard, trying to hear the stars. She had read somewhere, or heard on the radio, that black holes emit a sound too deep for humans to hear. She imagined it to be like a deep, deep French horn, or perhaps a whale song, calling across the universe, calling stars to come to it and enter, never to be seen again.

Whenever Bullitt stirred, Sirena told him more star child stories. She did not want him to leave. Some of the things he added, in embellishing her stories, might have been true about his own life. Sirena felt as though she was navigating a foreign shore in a small boat, trying to interpret the landmarks, fit them into the world as she knew it.

"Maybe …" said Sirena, "… maybe you have a twin star child. Another one like you."

"Or maybe we're all twins," he answered. "All the star children are clones."

"Nah ..." said Sirena. "That's too creepy. Who wants to think they are a clone?"

"You're right. I don't feel like one."

"But maybe this twin will show up one day and say, 'Hey bro! What's happening?'"

"But then will we have to go off and save the world?"

"Maybe you're supposed to save it right here. Like that mathematician who invented geometry. I don't remember his name. He figured out the circumference of the world by measuring the shadow of a stick in a well at noon, or something like that."

"That sounds vaguely familiar. Was it important?"

"I think so. At least it sounded important in school."

"What does this have to do with my clone, I mean, my twin?"

"Nothing. Except that maybe the mathematician's twin, his star child twin, came around and helped him out."

"Because the twin knew more?"

"Well, maybe he knew how to find his twin. And maybe between them, they knew enough."

Bullitt could not refute that.

Sirena thought that Bullitt's scar saved him from being too beautiful, but she was afraid to tell him so. Maybe later, she thought. She did not want to scare him away.

"You're not like anyone I have every met," she said.

"Aw, you say that to all the space aliens," he answered.

Sirena smiled and kissed him. He tasted like salt and popcorn, like innocence.

Later, Bullitt rose and began to dress.

"Where are you going?" she mumbled.

"I have to go to work in a couple of hours," he said.

"Isn't it Sunday?"

"I work half-days on Sunday."

"Mmmm," said Sirena.

He had to work that day, he said, as at his job in the financial district. Something about extra training. She imagined him, scrubbed and neck-tied, in one of the high rises on Figueroa. She tried to say goodbye, but she might have been asleep instead.

Sirena drifted on the paisley sheets until ten, then got up and stripped the bed and started a load of laundry. She straightened up Devi's apartment in anticipation of meeting her at the airport. Sirena was already rehearsing how she would tell Devi about Bullitt, imagining her reaction. At the same time, she was savoring the fact that he was hers alone right now, that no one knew about him, would not ask if she had heard from him.

He might have been a psycho killer, she thought, with those looks, another Ted Bundy. Her own loneliness had made her incautious. She wondered if her feeling of being alone was as great as that of the star children scattered across the universe. Did everyone look up at the stars and wonder who else was out there? If someone who would understand you and accept you without question might reside light-years away? Yes, there's God, but God will not hold you at night, stroke your hair and tell you stories, tell you how beautiful you are. Sirena was convinced that her more religious friends from high school just wanted to sleep with Jesus. Not that they would ever admit that, of course.

Sirena had started telling the star child stories to cover her own horror at the idea of a woman having her baby shot inside of her, but she thought the stories suited Bullitt. He seemed pleased with them, too. What she had really wanted to ask was, how his parents could stand to name him Bullitt. Did they really have such a dark sense of humor? Was the story he told about the scar even true? Maybe Bullitt wasn't his real name. Maybe, thought Sirena, as the lack of sleep began to give everything a glowing silhouette, she had imagined all of it. Her body told her otherwise.

The apartment clean, Sirena took a shower, dressed, put on her earrings and watch, and got in the car to pick up Devi from the airport. Had she been the one to meet Bullitt, Devi would have been much more skeptical. But last night his stories seemed real enough, not the sort of thing you would invent about yourself. Sirena moved into the new day with the sweet lethargy of the morning after, the unexpected gift of another person's body that sometimes precedes love.

A Hole in the Sky

The sun broke over the mountains like water running out of a pitcher. Tina touched her fingertips to high cheekbones where the first rays hit her, blinked away dazzles, and picked up the small blue leatherette suitcase. Trudging to the bus stop, battered tennies kicking up dust, she knew it would be hot today.

Tina took the bus to town. The driver knew her, saw her almost every day.

"You're up early. Taking a little trip?" he asked.

"Just visiting my aunt," she lied.

Tina looked straight ahead and found a seat by herself.

In Albuquerque she went to the Trailways station and waited for the office to open. There was an unease in her stomach, a buzzing in her head, but Tina fought it down. She tried to think of nothing, of gravel on the ground, of dirt on the roadway. She wished she was like dust—no name, no future, a cloud that could go where it wanted, do what it willed.

For sixty dollars Tina could go as far as Las Vegas; for ninety dollars she could go anywhere in the USA. Tina had one hundred and ten dollars, including the twenty her sister pressed into her hand as she let her silently out the door.

The bus rolled on, the open sky flawless, giving way to more open sky and highway and gas stations, and finally a big city and then another one. The landscape changed so little that it was easy for Tina to imagine that she sat still while the land and sky went scrolling past on giant rollers—unfurled ahead, taken up behind, to be repeated over and over again. Hadn't they passed that tree before? That gas station? Tina examined her nails and wished she had brought a magazine to look at.

Tina had heard once that the Hopi believed they had come out of a hole in the ground to live in this world, that there were other worlds below, dark, with no sun or moon. Spiderwoman had spun a web, and the other animals had climbed out—deer, coyote, roadrunner, bear. The first people had come out, too, clambering up the spiderweb to find the sun. Tina searched the relentless sky for a crack, a flaw she could crawl through to reach the fifth world. Some people thought this was the fifth world. It was too confusing. Everything was so unfair.

Tina ate candy bars and drank too-sweet pop and rinsed her face in bus station bathrooms. She wished her hair were short so that she could stick her head under a faucet and cool off.

"Malibu," she heard some teenagers say in Phoenix. "That's where the movie stars live." Tina had thought they lived in Hollywood or maybe Beverly Hills, where those blonde teenagers with straight teeth on television all went to school.

The bus reached Los Angeles, and Tina got off, almost forgetting her suitcase. It didn't have much in it anyway. She went in the bathroom and changed her shirt, taking the time to wash her armpits and face. An older woman came in and stared at her in her bra before she hurried into a fresh shirt.

"Don't mind her," said a Black girl who had just adjusted an elaborate wig and was now putting on mascara. "You have as much right to be here as she does."

Tina admired her new earrings in the dim mirror, plain silver hoops given to her by her sister, before leaving the bathroom.

Outside, Tina had no idea where to go. It was noisy and smelled bad. She watched the other people use phones or get in taxis or meet friends.

"Need a ride, darlin'?" drawled a man in a car the same color as her suitcase. "You look like you don't have no place to go."

"I'm going to Malibu," she declared in a voice that sounded shaky even to her.

The man put back his head and laughed. She could see the black fillings in his teeth.

"Tell you what. I'll give you a ride as far as Santa Monica, where I've got a little business."

Tina stood and stared at him. She was so tired she could barely focus her eyes.

"It's okay, darlin'. I'm just lookin' for someone to talk to. I can see that you're not interested in anything else."

What did it matter? thought Tina. She got in.

The man sold something that Tina did not understand. Office systems. She nodded and hugged the door. She wondered if she would live if she opened the door and jumped out. There were a lot of cars, a lot of city. No one would ever find her here, she thought.

Refusing money from the man, refusing to give him even her name, Tina got out in a place that smelled a little better. Instinctively, she walked west, toward the ocean. She found herself on a large walkway that went out over the water. It was crowded with families, and music blared from loudspeakers above the restaurants.

On a clear day, she heard a middle-aged man say to his wife, you can see Catalina Island.

Tina gazed at the uncertain sky beyond the dark, sparkling waters, but saw nothing. The water looked unreal to her like when Miss Esparza told them that the black, bubbly rock near their town was lava and had once been liquid. The light hurt her eyes. Tina resisted the urge to throw her suitcase out into the water off the pier and fling herself after it. She tried to keep her mind empty, to think of a drop of water falling into the ocean, a little something returning to a great nothing.

Tina walked back up the pier, which seemed a long way, longer than when she had come out, past souvenir shops, a food stand, an indoor carousel. She stood and watched a crowd of people watching some actors until she realized they were filming a commercial for the California lottery. They were using a trained pig. People were like pigs, thought Tina, and that was okay with everybody.

Tina walked off the pier, her suitcase feeling heavy, past whizzing athletic bodies in neon bathing suits on skates, and saw a small restaurant. It was dingy and neglected-looking with peeling beige paint on a stucco exterior. It reminded her of home. Tina wanted to sit down, so she went inside.

Tina felt heavy all over—her arms, her head, but especially the pit of her stomach. The uncertainty inside her felt like a black hole, a thousand stars smashed together so hard they made a hole in the sky, and Tina wanted to fall through the sky with it.

"Would you like a menu?" asked the waitress.

Tina realized she'd had her head down on her arms.

"Yes, please."

Tina took the plastic covered sheet in her hands and was suddenly ravenous.

"Would you like a glass of water?"

"Yes." She wondered if it would be extra.

"I'd like a hamburger and french fries, please."

Tina hadn't looked to see how much it cost. It didn't matter.

The waitress brought her silverware and ketchup.

Tina looked around for the first time. There were a few tables, a few booths, a counter, a cash register. An old-fashioned beer sign spilled electric water above the door to the kitchen. Instructions for performing the Heimlich maneuver were taped to the cash register. Tina stared at it dully. It was getting dark outside.

The waitress brought her food, and Tina ate greedily. As she was finishing, a movement in some bushes just past the parking lot caught her eye. It was a man, no, a boy her own age, huddled on the ground, his arms wrapped around his knees. He was shaking violently, as though freezing to death. He stared straight ahead, not seeing, just shaking and shaking as though his bones would fly apart and separate from the rest of his body.

Tina just stared, her french fries forgotten, until the waitress came over, and said, "Is everything okay?"

"There's something wrong with him," said Tina, pointing.

The waitress leaned over and looked out the window.

"Oh, my God," she said. "He must be on drugs. There's so many kids around here freaking out. I'll see what Fred wants to do. Are you through?"

Tina nodded, then regretted the two french fries she had left on her plate as the waitress hurried away.

The waitress bustled back out in a minute with the manager, and they both leaned over a booth to see the young man. He shook and shook, but his eyes looked dead, expressionless.

"Let's call the police," said Fred. "I don't want him dying out there."

"This town is just full of messed-up kids," said the waitress as she made out the check. "The city said it would protect the homeless, so they've come here from all over the state."

Tears welled up in Tina's eyes before her face crumpled like a newspaper.

"Oh, honey, I'm sorry," said the waitress. Her eyes rested on the battered suitcase for the first time, took in the long, dirty hair, the travel-stained jeans.

"I had no idea what I was saying. I always have such a big mouth. My God." She patted Tina on the shoulder and pulled a wad of tissues from her apron pocket and set them on the table.

"Do you have a place to stay tonight?"

Tina shook her head no. Greasy strands of hair fell before her eyes, and her nose began to run. She picked up the tissues and buried her face in them. Everything around her seemed red and hot, seemed to recede behind a roaring in her ears.

The waitress was talking to the manager.

"The police are sending an ambulance for that boy. Maybe they can take her to a shelter."

"The shelters are full by now," said the waitress. "This whole city's turning into a homeless shelter."

"Well, what do you want to do? She can stay until closing time. Ruth won't think much of me bringing her home."

The waitress came over to Tina.

"Honey, do you know anyone who can put you up?"

She shook her head. The wave of red had receded, and she was starting to be able to see again.

"Where are you from? Do you want to call someone to come for you?"

She started to say the name of her town, then shut her mouth. Her eyes focused on a silver ring the waitress wore, silver with a bit of turquoise.

"It's okay. I'll be okay," she finally said.

Two lines appeared between the waitress's eyes.

"We close at ten. Do you know anyone who could come get you? A relative? A friend?"

Tina continued to shake her head no, her eyes fixed on the edge of the table.

The waitress left.

She could hear her talking to Fred but could not understand what they were saying. Then she caught the word, "authorities."

Against her will, Tina's carefully blank mind began to remember. She saw his uniform, the flashing badge.

She remembered the cold, hard gravel biting into her knees when he'd made her get down on the ground, her earring coming loose, him pulling her head back roughly by her hair as she tried to reach for it, the bright hardware of his belt buckle as he'd taken down his pants. He'd had a big, irregular piece of turquoise in the buckle, real New Mexican turquoise like you can't get anymore.

The black hole in her stomach screamed and lurched.

Tina stood up and grabbed her suitcase.

"Let me pay for this, please," she said. "I'm okay. I just thought of someone."

The waitress and manager looked at each other.

"It's okay," she said, "I have money."

"Forget it," the waitress said. "It's my present to you."

Tina burst outside just as an ambulance, lights flashing, turned the corner.

She ran in the opposite direction, down toward the water again, which sparkled in the last, long rays of the sun.

She stopped at a paved trail that ran along the beach and continued to look west. It was the most beautiful thing she had ever seen—the sky all pink and orange, one perfect cloud, the sky directly above darkening to a deeper blue.

Tina wished she could just die now without resorting to any messy, painful violence. She wanted to set her suitcase down and keep walking. Maybe someone will just come up and kill me, she thought. The black hole in her middle screamed, a thousand dying suns falling toward the center of the universe.

What was it she needed to remember? The blood in the toilet, washing herself again and again, her father's face shutting like a metal door when he found out. She knew that she had died to him forever that day, that even if he looked, he would never see her again. It had been the missing earring that had given her away, that had forced her to confess, the spiral lizards given to her by her father on her fourteenth birthday. She still carried the other one with her. Tina pushed back the awful memories of the last few weeks and tried again.

Tina thought of the Hopi legend. Who had told it to her? Miss Esparza? One of the Indian kids? She tried hard to remember it.

There were no creatures in this world, no life. A hole opened up in the last world, and Spiderwoman spun a web to it. The animals climbed out—the deer, the bear, coyote, roadrunner. There were stories attached to each of these beginnings, but Tina did not know them. The first people climbed out and named themselves The People.

Big deal, Tina had thought at the tiime. That's like naming myself "me." I am me. It felt funny to think that; she had felt like nobody for so long.

She thought it again, there on the beach: I am me. I am Tina.

As she watched, a tiny pinpoint of light appeared high in the darkening sky. It flickered in and out of sight, then established itself surely and steadily as the sky deepened in color and the sun buried itself more securely under the blanket of ocean. The evening star? Venus, she thought. She had never seen it like this, never seen the sky meet the ocean. The possibility of a distance greater than the span of her native desert had never occurred to her before.

Tina imagined reaching up, inserting her fingertips in the tiny hole made by the star, and working them through—then her arms, then her face and body; wriggling through to a place that was warm and soft and silent, lying peacefully on the new ground as the other animals, who could still talk, gathered around: the deer not yet afraid of coyote, the elk not yet jealous of bear. They were not yet enemies, not yet hiding and fighting and tricking each other. The world was only just possible, not yet done.

The street lights came on, and Tina blinked and looked around. A glitter on the ground caught her eye.

Stooping to look more closely, she saw that it was a shiny, silver earring. Grabbing for her pocket, Tina fumbled in it and pulled out its twin, a silver lizard curled in a loop. She picked up the other and held them both in her hands.

Tina looked back up at the star, and the different lights seemed to spin around her. Maybe this is the fifth world, she thought. Maybe I fell through somehow. I name this world "California."

Tina picked up her suitcase and started back up the hill, each footstep touching the new ground until she came to the place where she had gotten out of the blue car. She could see more light just up ahead, growing brighter as she drew closer. It opened up to a shopping area with lots of people walking, outdoor restaurants, bookstores. Tina watched these new people carefully; everyone seemed to glow with a special light. She sat down on a planter and touched the cement beside her carefully. It was still warm from the day, a gift from the fifth sun.

Tina grasped the earrings hard in her hand, her promise of miracles yet untold, until they almost cut, and began to breath more easily.

After awhile she noticed a neon sign in the shape of a jolly bear. Camping gear? Ice cream? She could not tell what kind of a store it was, but she was pulled closer by the familiar shape. At the door was posted a "Help Wanted" sign. She could hear laughter coming from the doorway. Tina was drawn forward into the circle of warm light, and reaching out her fingertips, she stepped inside.

Crater the Earth

"What about an Indian Reservation?"

"Nah, they mostly sell the safe and sane stuff here in California. You can get fireworks in Tijuana or Rosarita that will crater the earth."

Luther said this with a certain authority, as though he did this all the time. He leaned against the side of his pickup, shifting a plastic straw from one corner of his mouth to the other. About Sirena's height, Luther tended to wear a black *Close Encounters of the Third Kind* t-shirt and was almost as wide as he was tall.

Luther was one of Bullitt's friends, but Sirena wasn't sure how they knew each other. The bank? Maybe Luther was a security guard.

"I'm making a run next weekend, if you want me to pick some up," he said.

"Sure," said Bullitt. "Let me give you some cash." He pulled out some twenties and handed them to Luther, who stuffed them in his front pocket without looking at them. Sirena wondered if Bullitt would ever see the money again, or the fireworks, but he did not seem concerned.

A week later they drove out to the high desert, past where Sirena's parents lived, then into the mountains from the back side. They followed a rough track around a No Trespassing sign full of holes and a couple of posts with a desultory chain hung between them.

"Where are we?" asked Sirena as Bullitt pulled off to one side next to some trucks. They seemed to be driving the only sedan.

"It's an old gravel pit from when they built the highway through Cajon Pass. It's a good place to shoot off a few fireworks without bothering anyone."

As they got out of the car, they could hear a car radio playing heavy metal. Then a deep boom knocked them back.

"Maybe I should have brought earplugs," said Sirena, grimacing. She wondered why she had agreed to this. Devi had told her she should get out more, be open to new experiences.

"Don't worry about it," said Bullitt. "If it's too loud, we can just step back."

Bullitt headed up a footpath that skirted the raw gorge of a deepening and widening pit. It opened up into a box canyon where backhoes had clawed away the flanks in order to loosen gravel. Dirt and rocks lay about in rough mounds, their edges beginning to soften with time and weather. Toward the back was a high, level area where people were setting up their explosives. In front of it was a deep, black pool of water. Sirena could not tell if the staging area had been there or had been created by the pyroheads for their own uses.

Luther met them there. "Where you been?" he asked.

"No point in coming early," said Bullitt. "You can't see anything before it's dark."

"Yeah, but the sound, man," said Luther, grinning evilly. "That booty-shakin' boom when you stand too close." His gaze lingered on Sirena.

Sirena tried to laugh but wondered if Luther had any hearing left. The smell of gunpowder and marijuana drifted across the pit.

"What did you get?" asked Bullitt.

"Good stuff, my man, starting with a little paca lolo." He lit a hand-rolled cigarette and after taking a deep pull, handed it to Bullitt, who smelled it before partaking. He handed it to Sirena, who held it for a few seconds, turning away from them, before handing it back to Luther.

As her eyes adjusted to the dark, Sirena could make out some of the other participants. They were dressed mostly in black with pale hands and faces. Some were cadaverously thin with jewelry glinting in their faces. Others were like Luther, broad with fast food and beer. They stood and sat around the loose edge of the gravel pit, facing the impromptu stage.

"Then there's this," said Luther. He walked over to his truck and climbed into the bed, where he pulled back a filthy blue plastic tarp. Bullitt climbed in after him, and they began handing out small cardboard boxes to Sirena, all marked Glorious Group/Hecho en China. Sirena took each one and made a neat stack on the ground.

They all turned as the next set of fireworks went off. Several low, rumbling booms were followed by thousands of small firecrackers and finally by an aerial show of fountains and sprays.

"Too light," said Bullitt, "that was a waste of time."

Sirena noticed that the people standing around seemed completely at ease handling the explosives, as though they did this all the time—a little world of creatures in black t-shirts and face studs who made things go "whoomp!" in the night.

As they waited their turn to set up, Luther produced another mj cigarette. This time Sirena refused to even hold it in solidarity, but they didn't seem to care.

"Go to Burning Man this year?" asked Bullitt.

"Yeah, for about a day," said Luther. "I've got some friends who live for it all year." He shrugged. "It's getting sort of corporate, like everything else. Too many rules."

When Sirena stepped back involuntarily at one of the explosions, Bullitt caught her by each arm from behind. She relaxed into him, and his arms went around her. When he began caressing her breasts, she grew uneasy and twisted away.

Sirena turned, startled, and found herself facing a grinning Luther.

"Steady there," he said. "You don't want to turn an ankle, or we'll have to carry you out."

Sirena made a fist and socked him in the jaw, knocking him back a couple of steps. Bullitt looked at her curiously as she walked away for a moment, then came and stood on the other side of him. Luther stood there rubbing his face.

They watched an intensely colorful display.

"Filipino works," said Luther.

After awhile, as if the patterns burning themselves onto her tortured retinas were finally penetrating to her brain, Sirena understood what was going on. In this ragged setting, an abandoned construction site lined with trash and broken beer bottles, this was art. As a deafening silence closed in after the display, Sirena began to clap. Alone at first, she was soon joined by others. It was now dark enough to actually see something. The artist, a girl in a *Pinky and the Brain* t-shirt and black fishnets bowed with a flourish before yielding to the next show. The mood shifted as the mole-like creatures acknowledged each other.

At last, it was their turn. Luther directed Sirena and Bullitt as they set up the cakes and mortars, rockets and fountains festooned with strings of tiny firecrackers, like bristly duct tape. Luther rigged everything together with lengths of what looked like thick, rough string that he spooled out from a reel. Then Bullitt and Sirena scrambled back to the pickup while Luther picked up the end of the fuse and lit it with his stub, turning his back like a matador while he strolled confidently back to join them.

The first boom shook the ground beneath them. The second started a landslide on the far side of the pit, where a few people stood on a narrow ledge. They swore and scrambled up to safer ground.

The third boom knocked them all flat, Sirena certain they had triggered an earthquake on the San Andreas fault and would die here, buried alive. But it was rapidly followed by a ground display of earth flowers, desert roses, prickly pears and barrels. Pink blooms within green, red within lime, some displays lingering while others burst over them in frenzies of little patterns. Then a piercing assembly of Piccolo Petes and screaming eagles followed. Low fountains filled the air with whines and whistles, tiny lights and large ones blooming rapidly into the next, and the next. Sirena's head danced. She could not see her hands or her feet. Only the lights in front of her on the pagan altar.

The ground show dissipated, and people came out of their involuntary crouches, a stance they had unconsciously assumed when the first mortars went off, poised to run. A single fountain began, white, a pale column rising into the night like an apparition. Sirena tried to remember what the hologram of Princess Leia said in *Star Wars*. Help me, Obi-Wan Kenobi? The column was joined by two more, one blue, one green. A tiny light went on and off to her left. Sirena looked over and realized that Luther was timing the display. It was all clockwork.

As the three columns rose, the crowd pressed closer, as though irresistably drawn toward the light.

Then a hundred fountains kicked in, and the crowd stepped back again, as much to see the top, where the fountains were exploding well above the lip of the canyon. The sheriff could probably see it, too, and they would all be fined if caught. Bullitt stood behind Sirena, his arms wrapped around her. Luther stood apart and smoked, his eyes half open behind his glasses, a professional admiring his own work.

The last, transcendent lights faded from the sky. A lone voice called out, "Awesome," followed by a round of whistles and cheers. People began to drift away to their vehicles, and Sirena heard the first engine start up, the tires crunching down the gravel track, a single bottle bursting beneath a tire. Suddenly, Luther's truck started, and Sirena and Bullitt stepped away from behind it. Luther raised his hand in the rearview mirror and drove away.

"Not much for goodbyes, huh?"

"He has to work," said Bullitt.

The sky was lightening. Sirena realized that the false dawn had begun. Bullitt began to squint at the photos he had taken. "Nothing," he said. "I might as well have propped a flashlight in my closet and taken pictures of it."

He looked up at Sirena, who was watching the sky. "Go sit over there."

"Where?" she asked. "Up there?"

"Yeah."

"Is it safe now?"

"Probably."

Sirena walked the narrow, crumbling trail to the raised area, which was about waist-high to her. She gingerly placed her hands on it and swung her knee up, brushing her hands on her jeans as she picked her way across the spent shells and cooling debris. Sirena did not feel tired. Rather, she felt oddly light and refreshed, as though she, too, could go straight to work if she had to.

Sirena made her way to the center of the makeshift stage, where most of the fireworks had been placed.

She felt like a sacrifice, a burnt offering. She sat down on the trashed ground. Nestling her bottom into the grit and ashes, she crossed her legs and pressed her bare ankles into the filthy residue. Everything smelled like gunpowder. As a ray of light cut into the canyon from the east, it touched her face, and she lifted up her eyes. Like one of Devi's goddesses, she turned her hands palms up and touched each thumb to each second finger. Smoke and dust became visible around her as the sunlight increased.

Bullitt captured her, the first image of the night he could keep.

Sirena crawled out of bed at noon the next day. Her phone was flashing with messages from Devi.

"Where you been, girl?" asked Devi when Sirena called her back.

"Oh, we got back early this morning. Maybe six."

Sirena pulled open her living room blinds. The bright sunshine hurt her eyes, and the trees in the courtyards were swaying back and forth.

"You go with that rasty Luther?"

"Yeah, we met him there. How do you know Luther?"

"I've just heard you talk about him."

"He tried to hit on me last night."

"Oh, my. Big surprise. What did you do?"

"I hit him. Not as hard as I wanted to. No big deal."

"What did Bullitt say?"

"Nothing. I don't even think he noticed."

"Hmmm. Did you have fun?"

"It was okay. Interesting in a weird way. These pyros who spend all their time and money on fireworks."

"They need a ritual," said Devi. "Fireworks are how you get the attention of the gods."

"It was ritualistic. Maybe that's what made it more interesting than just bright lights and loud noises. Although, I may be deaf for a couple of days."

Sirena made herself coffee and started a load of laundry. The weatherman predicted Santa Ana winds, and she was glad she hadn't bothered to wash her car the previous weekend.

Sirena called her mother.

"Are you coming out?"

"Not this weekend, mom, maybe next."

"Aye, mija, we never see you!"

"I was planning to visit last week, but you were out."

"Pues, Dad wanted to go to the RV show."

"I'll call Abuela and see if she needs anything. I have to get groceries, anyway."

Sirena called her grandmother. After six or seven rings, she answered.

"Hello, Abuela," said Sirena.

Her grandmother expressed much delight at the call.

"Do you need anything at the store?"

"Sí. Pero no mas leche para mi cafecito."

"No problem. I'll bring it in about an hour."

"Pero tienes cuidado," she said. "Esta poniendo vientoso los Santa Anas."

"Oh, right," said Sirena. "The wind. I heard it on TV. I'll be careful!"

By the time Sirena got into her car, it was gusty. Although she turned her back to it, Sirena got grit in her eyes while getting out of her car in the supermarket parking lot. By the time she got to her grandmother's, a steady wind was blowing out of the east. Her grandmother had taken Patito inside and put him in the bathtub.

Sirena gave her grandmother the two little cans of evaporated milk that she made last for two weeks in her coffee but didn't sit down.

"I have to go, Grandma," she said. "I still have to put my clothes in the dryer."

Sirena picked up a latte and a bagel on her way home. The sky had turned muddy with swirling dust.

On the hour, the news included an item about fires in the mountains, but there were no details. By evening, two fires were still out of control, one in San Diego County and one in the San Bernardino Mountains. Sirena called her parents, but they did not answer.

"It's a mess, babe," said Bullitt when he called. "We got out of there just in time."

"What happened?"

"One of those fires is in the area where we were last night. The sheriff is calling it possible arson."

"Are they … looking for people?"

"You bet. Turn on the news."

Sirena pulled her portable television out of the hall closet and plugged it in. Helicopters hovered above the glowing forest, buffeted by the strong winds, as they tried to drop retardant into the steep canyons. A reporter in a red parka did a stand-up from Big Bear.

"A fire of suspicious origin is racing up the east side of the San Bernardino Mountains toward this resort community. So far, there have been no evacuation orders, but the authorities are on alert. The fires have been aggravated by the Santa Ana winds gusting up to sixty-five miles per hour. We will update at 11:00."

Sirena turned off the TV and curled up on the couch. Could they really have started the fire? Everything around them had seemed rocky and barren. Only if sparks had flown out of the canyon could they have sparked some brush.

What had they left behind? she wondered. Burned-out fireworks shells, probably still smoking. Plenty of evidence in the form of beer cans, tire tracks, and cigarette butts, things with DNA on them. Plus, Luther had marijuana, not that everyone else didn't. Would they test the lips of every person in Southern California? She didn't even know who the rest of those people were.

The following day, Monday, Bullitt called her at work.

"Luther didn't come in today. They say he's been taken in for questioning on suspicion of possession of illegal fireworks and possible arson."

"What should we do?" asked Sirena. She stood to ease the door to her tiny office closed. "Anything?"

"Just hang tight. We didn't do anything."

"But we were there."

"Yeah, a lot of people were there."

"Do you think someone turned Luther in?"

"Maybe. I don't know. That photo of you I took?"

"Yeah?"

"It was fantastic. You looked ecstatic, like you were having an out of body experience."

"Really? More like an 'I've been up all night' experience. You'll have to show it to me."

By that evening they were evacuating Wrightwood, and Sirena's mother was packing.

"Your Dad says he won't leave."

"He'll have to, if the fire department evacuates. What does he think?" This had happened a couple of times before, but Sirena's parents had never been forced to leave.

"He says he'll stand on the roof with the garden hose. He says if he can keep it wet, the fire won't take it."

"Well, just be ready, Mom, and let me know what happens."

"We were thinking, mija ..."

"What?"

"If we evacuate, can we stay with you?"

"I guess so. You know how small my place is. What about Aunt Julia?"

"Cepo hasn't been well. He was just in the hospital for awhile, so I don't want to bother her."

"Sure, Mom. It would just be for a couple of days, if it happens at all."

"I guess I'll go ahead and pack for your Dad, too. Just in case."

When Sirena went to bed, she dreamed that she was a young teen, thirteen years old. She left her friends, including Kerby, that rotten kid who always put his hands all over the girls, to return home for something. It took her a long time to get home, cutting through people's yards, backtracking once because the path that ran by the trailer park was too muddy. The last long street, she rollerskated uphill, then pumped her arms at the top like an Olympic athlete. But she had made it. A mysterious boy was coming down the street at the same time, someone she did not recognize. What had she forgotten? She woke just as she was going up the front walk to the sound of her apartment intercom.

It was 6:00 a.m.

"We're here, mija. We had to leave."

Sirena remembered the fire. "Oh, Mom. Why didn't you call when you left? Come on in." She released the main door to the apartments and pulled on her sweats and sneakers. By then they were in the hall.

Her arms spilling half-full grocery bags and suitcases, Sirena's mother collapsed into the living room. "I'm so scared," she sobbed. "Everything's on fire."

"What about the house? Is it okay?"

Sirena's father came in and sat wearily on the couch. He placed his hat on the coffee table and threw a bag of golf clubs on the floor. He didn't golf, but someone had given him an expensive set of clubs.

"Were you up all night?"

"Yes, we were too worried to sleep." Sirena's mother took off two layers of coats, exuding an air of smoke and upset. She opened a voluminous purse and extracted her Chihuahua dog, Peppy. The dog barked once and shook his tiny body at the joy of being freed. Sirena's apartment did not allow pets, but she figured if the manager said anything, she would explain it was an emergency.

Sirena's father had stretched out on the couch and fallen asleep.

"I'll help you bring things in. How much more is there?"

"Just a few things. Most of it can stay in the car. I'll get them."

"No, just give me the keys. Then I can put your car in a visitor's spot. Do you want coffee? Or do you want to sleep?"

"I'll make some coffee for you. I know you have to go to work."

"What about the house?"

"It was okay when we left. They just made everybody get out. A fireman came to the door."

A gray pall hung over the city when Sirena drove to work. Her eyes felt gritty and dry. At the office, people talked of nothing but the Santa Ana winds and the fires. Agents stayed in the office, trying to look busy, loathe to go out and try to sell anything in this weather.

"Luther's cooperating with the authorities," said Bullitt on the phone.

"What does that mean? He must be telling them something."

"There were a lot of people there that night."

"Including us."

"Luther's a smart guy."

Sirena remembered his hands on her. She remembered how it felt when she hit him. She had held back just before connecting, afraid to break his jaw over nothing, and shuddered.

"What?"

"Nothing. I just … never mind."

"About Luther?"

"I just remembered a dream I had."

"About what?"

"Something creepy."

"Meet me tonight?"

"My parents are staying with me. They got evacuated from their house."

"They came all the way out here? Won't they put them up in a motel or something?"

"I don't know. It should just be for a day or two. They've got their dog with them."

"Really? What kind?"

"I've got to go." Sirena hung up the phone. She didn't really like talking to Bullitt on the phone, especially at work. She preferred running her hands over him, the black hair, the smooth skin, the scar. If she could just rub the scar enough, maybe she could make it go away, smooth it back into the perfection of his skin.

Nobody wanted to go out for lunch, so one of the agents brought back sandwiches. They ate in the break room next to Sirena's office.

"I hear they have some suspects in the Cajon Pass fire," said Wyatt between bites of Philly sandwich. "Some Goth types."

"Goth types? Like Satanic rituals?" asked Gloria. She was eating orange Jello out of a tiny container.

"I don't know. People with tattoos."

"That doesn't mean they're satanic."

"Sirena's a little more open-minded than the rest of us."

This was a reference to the girl Sirena was helping with her GED. She was from New Mexico and had run away from home to California. Sometimes she came into the office with Sirena, just to see what an office was like.

Sirena decided this was a good time to change the subject. "They evacuated Del Rosa. My parents are staying with me."

"Really? It's come that far?"

"I think it's mostly because of the smoke. They don't want people passing out in their houses." Sirena had just made that up. She couldn't bear the idea that their house might really go up in flames.

At home, Sirena's mother had washed out her nylons and hung them all over the bathroom. She was frying fish sticks for dinner. There were stacks of canned "Pepper Pot" soup on the counter. Sirena's father sprawled on the same couch where he had fallen asleep, still looking red-eyed with fatigue, watching the news. He hadn't shaved. Sirena's apartment looked like a bomb shelter.

After dinner Sirena moved some stuff and pulled the Murphy bed out of the wall. She and her mom had slept there last night, her father on the couch. Peppy slept wherever he wanted. The television stayed on the whole time, footage of burning houses and trees, interviews with fire chiefs, with angry residents.

"The winds have abated enough to use helicopters for dropping fire retardants," said a reporter. "The authorities expect the fires to be under control by midnight."

"Let's go," said her father, standing suddenly.

"Where?" said Sirena's mother. She was in her robe, putting her hair in foam rollers.

"Home."

"Now? It's late."

"There might be looters."

"Well, just give me five minutes." Sirena's mother pulled out her rollers and began to gather her things. Her father put on his coat and hat and picked up his golf clubs.

"At least your golf clubs are safe," said Sirena, smiling.

"Listen," said her father, starting to get angry. Then he smiled sheepishly. "Don't start with me," he said, shaking his finger at her.

"Let's go for a ride. You want to go for a ride, Peppy?"

The Chihuahua jumped willingly into the oversized bag she held open for him.

Sirena helped them carry things downstairs. She couldn't believe the things her mother had brought—mostly food.

"Call me when you get there. Okay?" she said.

An hour later the phone rang. "You'll never believe it," said her mother.

"What?"

"The house. The block behind us is gone. Some people lost everything, everything. Even their cars. But our house is fine. You can see the burn marks on the back fence. It's a miracle, like an angel was protecting us."

Sirena sat down on the bed, suddenly exhausted. "I'm glad, Mom."

"Sorry to call so late."

"It's okay, I asked you to call. I'll try to visit next weekend."

"Okay, honey. Bye."

Just as she was dozing off, Bullitt called.

"They let everyone go."

"What are you talking about?"

"The arson. The fire."

"Yeah?"

"For lack of evidence."

"Good," Sirena sighed. "I'm really tired."

"You know that photo of you? The one we took at the gravel pit?"

"Yes?"

"It was fantastic."

"You already told me that."

"I deleted it."

"Why?"

"Evidence."

"Well, then I'll never know how fantastic it was," murmured Sirena.

"Nope. We were never there."

"Where?"

"No where."

Boardwalk

Sirena and Bullitt met at the Santa Monica boardwalk, leaving their cars in the lot while they walked down the length of the beach, dodging in-line skaters in Spandex. On the way back, they detoured into the shopping area to look for ice cream. A cheerful bear beckoned to them from the neon shape that enclosed it.

"Frosty Bear, Frosty Bear, why'd you fill my ice cream with hair?" sang Bullitt.

"Ewww ..." responded Sirena, and slapped him on the arm.

A glass case full of brightly colored ice cream buckets stretched out before them, and it took awhile to consider the merits of Mocha Almond Fudge, Totally Tropical, Banana Blitz, and Kool Mint Kraze. Sirena settled on one scoop of Jamaica Mocha and one of You're So Vain Vanilla while Bullitt took a double scoop of Caffeine Crash.

"You'll be up all night," said Sirena.

"Mmmm ... would you like that?" asked Bullitt.

Sirena giggled, but did not answer him.

"I like your earrings," she said to the girl behind the counter.

Startled, the girl grabbed one of her earrings as though it might be missing. "Thanks," she said, seemingly reassured. The sides of her head were shaved, and the top braided back down the center of her head. She had a silver bar in one nostril.

"Do you know her?" asked Bullitt outside.

"No, but now that I think about it, she looks familiar. Wait." Sirena stopped walking. "Isn't she the girl who jumped on your car hood that night?"

"How should I know? I barely saw her. Suddenly, these shoes jump on the car out of nowhere and bail off the other side. Scared me, I tell you." Bullitt bit at his ice cream cone as it began to melt. "Still have dents in the hood."

"I recognized the earrings. The lizard shape," said Sirena. "I think that man was chasing her."

It had been after a movie, and they had just pulled out of the parking lot. After the noise of her feet hitting the car, the shape of a body hunched, balanced on her hands for a moment before she jumped off again, her breath quick and labored. Sirena and Bullitt had instinctively looked down the alley in the direction from which the girl had come. All they could see was a dark shape walking toward them. He had not seemed to be in a hurry.

"Let's get out of here!" Sirena had said, and Bullitt had jammed the car into gear and floored it.

"Could be," said Bullitt. "Hard to say what people do with their time off."

They sat down on a planter while shoppers and strollers streamed past them. Their colorful bags advertised the stores where they had purchased clothes and shoes. A teenager in dirty blonde dreadlocks sat on the sidewalk in front of a Chinese restaurant and panhandled until the proprietor came out and shooed him away. He squatted, disconsolate, in a doorway a few yards away.

"I can't imagine trying to live on the street," said Sirena.

"Some of them do it for laughs," said Bullitt. "Their moms and dads are just up the street in million-dollar houses."

"Not all of them. I had a girlfriend who started running away from home in junior high," said Sirena.

"Why?"

"Her stepdad beat her. Did stuff to her."

"I guess there are worse things than being homeless," said Bullitt. "Good thing no one in California is homeless."

"That's right. That was the first time you told me that!"

‡‡‡

After their encounter with the hood jumper, they had gotten on the freeway with difficulty. There had been so much traffic, it had been impossible to merge until a truck driver gave them a break.

"Where are all these people going at this hour?" said Sirena.

"They have to be out of their houses and apartments," said Bullitt.

"Why?" asked Sirena.

"Because other people live in them while they're gone."

"What?"

"Sure. At any given time," said Bullitt, "twenty percent of the population of California has to be on the freeway, so that other people can live in their houses. Otherwise, there wouldn't be enough housing for everyone. When they go home, the people in their apartments and houses have to get on the freeway. They think it's their house and don't know the other people live there."

"Is this true for everyone?" asked Sirena. "Is someone in my place right now?"

"Probably," said Bullitt. "You know those times you can't find your sunglasses, or something, and when you do find them, they're someplace you would never put them?"

"That's someone else who moved them?"

"Absolutely."

"Wow. That's brilliant!" said Sirena. "That explains a lot. I may never look at my apartment the same way again."

They pulled into the parking lot at Bullitt's apartment and went inside.

"That even explains who bought your furniture," said Sirena, setting her purse on the couch that appeared to be covered in orange shag carpeting.

"Unfortunately, it still showed up on my credit card," said Bullitt. "What do you mean, don't you like my stuff?"

"Well, it's, it's …" Sirena turned, gesturing at the lava lamps and black shelving that was fixed randomly to the walls. Bullitt's Pez dispenser collection decorated the low, dark coffee table. "So retro. Like something from the sixties, maybe, except I don't know if they made furniture like this."

"I ordered it all from a catalogue," Bullitt admitted. "If I ordered a thousand dollars worth of stuff, they delivered free."

"And did you consult with the other people who live here?" asked Sirena.

"No, but the catalogue came to this apartment when I first moved here. So they, or he, must have ordered it," said Bullitt.

Sirena kicked off her shoes and sat on the couch. Then she moved and sat on a black chair, putting her feet up on a matching ottoman.

"A thousand dollars," she said. "Once I pay off my college loans, I could move to an unfurnished place and buy my own furniture."

"Or you could move here," said Bullitt.

"Too far from work," said Sirena. She tried not to think what he meant by saying that.

"But closer to me," said Bullitt, sitting on the arm of the chair, then squeezing down beside Sirena.

"Are you serious?" she asked.

"Sure," he said. "Why not?"

"Well, for one thing, no one even knows I'm seeing you. And for another, I have no idea who you are. Who your people are."

Part of Sirena was in a panic. She knew her parents would never approve of the arrangement.

"Well, we'll have to do something about that." He kissed her.

"And what about the other people who live here?" said Sirena. "You think it's another guy? What if he doesn't like me?"

"Well, he'll have to get someone your size to move in with him."

"To share my clothes?"

"Sure. Then you'll have twice as many clothes."

Sirena told Bulllitt about the night when, as a little girl, she had seen an apparition. She was not often scared, but sometimes wind or strange noises woke her up, and the friendly room with its white walls and colorful pictures seemed strangely distorted, as though she was not really awake. Sirena was always too scared to get out of bed and tell someone.

That particular night she heard strange noises in the ceiling above her and was sure a burglar was breaking in through the roof. Sirena prayed as hard as she could for God to protect her. When she opened her eyes, a blue figure was hovering in the air above her, a woman who assured Sirena that she was safe, that she was always being watched over. It must have been her guardian angel, she thought, or a blue fairy, like in *Pinocchio*.

"I felt better," said Sirena, "and I actually went to sleep after that, but I always felt like," she shrugged, "I had peeked behind the scenery in some way. You know what I mean?"

That was the way Bullitt made her feel sometimes, that things are going on all the time that we have no knowledge about.

"Sure," said Bullitt. "The blue light lady."

"You know her?"

Bullitt shrugged. "Just in passing. If you had been raised a Catholic, you would have called her the Virgin Mary."

Sirena hadn't thought of that. "Were you? I mean, are you Catholic?"

"No ..." he said slowly. "My parents are Eastern Orthodox. Far Eastern. Far-out Eastern Orthodox. With a little shamanism thrown in."

Sirena never knew when he was joking.

Bullitt got up and opened the sliding glass door to his balcony. The smell of marijuana floated in on the night air.

"That's Sheila," he said. "She lives upstairs."

Bullitt came back and carefully gathered up the Pez dispensers from his coffee table, putting them on the couch. He lay down on the table, his hands crossed on his chest, his feet next to Sirena on the chair. He looked perfectly comfortable, as though he often reclined there. The low light made him look bronzed.

"My parents' main belief, as far as I can tell, is that there is more to life than we see."

"Like other people living in our apartments?"

"Or jumping on the hoods of our cars."

Bullitt raised an arm like Tutankhamun delivering a blessing from beyond the grave and revealed the Wonder Woman Pez dispenser nestled in the palm of his hand.

Surbia

The day Bullitt asked Sirena if she wanted to visit his parents took her completely by surprise.

"I didn't know your parents lived here," she said. She had known Bullitt for about six months, ever since they had sat next to each other during the Festival of Animated Shorts in Venice Beach.

"Sure. I grew up here," he said. "They still live in the same house."

"I guess I always thought you were from some place else," she said.

Bullitt drove east on I-10, then south into a neighborhood Sirena had never seen, near Disneyland. When they exited the freeway, there were rows and rows of small well-kept houses punctuated by blocks of faceless apartment complexes. Sirena recognized it as one of the small cities on the periphery of Los Angeles that was full of immigrant populations—Cambodian, Russian, Indian, and Mexican—who proclaimed their arrival on billboards advertising restaurants and insurance services. The area was such a mishmash, Sirena might have once driven through it on the way to somewhere else, but could not remember. It was what her boss, Sonny, at the real estate agency, would have called "Surbia." When a listing became available in a place like Westchester or Anaheim, east or southeast of Los Angeles, he usually swapped it to another agency in exchange for a property located farther north.

Bullitt pulled into the driveway of a low, beige house with a red tile roof. An older woman knelt in the yard, tilling her garden with an oversized spoon.

"Kadarchy!" she yelled, struggling to her feet with difficulty. She wore an old-fashioned bib apron tied back over her dress. She and Bullitt embraced and spoke in a language Sirena did not recognize.

"My mother," said Bullitt, presenting the woman with dark, slanted eyes and flushed cheeks. Sirena shook her hand while the woman nodded, smiling, and they went inside.

There, a heavy-set man in a big chair watched television in the darkened room.

"My father," said Bullitt.

The man stood and took Sirena's hand in both of his. "Call me Alex," he said, bowing slightly. "Pleased to meet you."

Bullitt's mother brought out Kool-Aid and thick slices of pound cake, then sat on a straight back chair near the door to the kitchen, fanning herself with the skirt of her flowered apron.

Bullitt's father smiled at Sirena. "You like sports?" he shouted. He had been watching soccer on television.

"Sometimes," said Sirena. "Anything but football."

"You don't like futbol?" said Alex.

Bullitt said something to his father. "I explained that you didn't mean soccer. You didn't, did you?"

Sirena shook her head no, smiling.

"Sometimes soccer is called football."

That exchange seemed to have exhausted Alex's English, or at least his attention. Sirena ate pound cake from a plate in her lap, trying not to drop crumbs, while Bullitt walked around with his mother. She seemed to want him to fix something in the kitchen. From her seat Sirena could see the corner of a table through the kitchen doorway, covered in bright oil cloth and stacked with clean white dishes. Sirena looked around the living room. The walls were painted a rather dark blue and were studded with small paintings, artificial flowers, and an old, flat-looking painting of a dark-skinned Mary holding the baby Jesus. Mary wore a red shawl that seemed to float around her head, edged in gold, and both mother and child had perfectly round halos behind their heads. The Mary in the painting was very different from the Virgin of Guadalupe depictions Sirena was used to seeing everywhere, yet strangely compelling in her own way.

Sirena listened while Bullitt talked to his mother in their strange language—like Russian, thought Sirena. Or not at all like Russian. What did she know? All she could tell was that it was not Spanish, French, Italian, Portuguese, any Filipino dialect, Chinese, Japanese, Korean, Hmong, or Lao. Those were all languages she heard spoken on the streets of L.A. on a regular basis, coming out of the mouths of people who seemed to match up.

The television was set into a wall of shelves that held numerous framed photos, large and small. She recognized what must have been Bullitt's high school graduation picture—one of those where they airbrush out all of your stray hairs and do things to your eyebrows. Bullitt was wearing a coat and tie. The word "icon" strayed into her mind, and Sirena glanced over at the Mary and Jesus on the wall. The painting looked like an icon. Sirena had never seen Bullitt in a tie, although she knew he wore one to work as a bank teller.

As her eyes scanned the family photos, Sirena glanced furtively at Bullitt's father, trying to find a resemblance. When he caught her eye, he smiled broadly.

Bullitt's mother stepped back into the room, putting something in her pocket.

"What?" said Alex, sitting up. "What is that?"

The woman lowered her head and shook it.

Bullitt stepped out of the kitchen close behind her."It's nothing, Dad."

"What? Let me see." The older man stood, strode over to his wife, and held out his hand.

Reluctantly, she withdrew hers from her apron pocket. In it were two twenty-dollar bills.

Bullitt's father took them from her, impatiently, as though she were a child. "Is that all?" he demanded. His genial mood had vanished.

"That's all, Dad. I just want her to be able to get a little something for herself now and then."

Alex held the money out to Bullitt until he was forced to take it. "I take care of her myself," he said. "I always have. We don't need it."

There was no hint of thanks in his voice. Sirena glimpsed the hurt and frustration in Bullitt's eyes as he took the money.

Sirena, embarrassed for them, did not know where to look. Her own mother held a series of part-time jobs over the years, so she always had her own money. And now her own Social Security check.

"Keep your money," said Bullitt's father. "Spend it on her," he said, brusquely motioning at Sirena.

Sirena's embarrassment turned to anger. She stood and walked to the kitchen to put down her plate. "I need to get back," she said, addressing no one in particular.

Bullitt's mother broke from the tableau and took Sirena's plate from her with an apologetic smile. She seemed anxious to put some distance between herself and her husband.

"Thanks so much," Sirena said to her. "It was delicous."

At the door Bullitt's father, again affable, had one more word for Sirena. He stood in the doorway and put his hand on her arm. "Handsome," he said to Bullitt.

"Beautiful," corrected Bullitt, smiling. "She is beautiful."

"Sexy," added Alex.

Sirena looked at the ground, anxious now to leave.

In the car Sirena looked at Bullitt, searching for his parents' features in his face.

"I didn't know you grew up speaking a different language," she said.

"Nope," he said, "not a word of English, or almost not a word, until I started school."

"Sports," said Sirena.

"Handsome," said Bullitt, then, "Beautiful." He reached over and took Sirena's hand. "You are definitely beautiful."

"Who was the other boy in that photo with you?" asked Sirena.

"You mean, Kyle?"

"I guess so. The boy with lighter hair."

"He's my cousin. My aunt and her family live here, too. My Dad works for her husband, who is American."

"Ah. Handsome."

"Beautiful."

"So you're an only child?"

"I told you. They couldn't have more after me," he said, evenly.

Bullitt's mother had been shot, he had told her, during a robbery while pregnant with him. Bullitt had been delivered by emergency C-section.

"They put her back together after delivering me but told her not to try to have more children."

Sirena watched his face as he said this. "But how could they stand to name you Bullitt? That would make me so sad to call my son by the thing that almost killed him."

Bullitt was quiet for awhile as he drove the side streets back to the freeway. Sirena worried that maybe she should not have asked about this.

"There's some Mongolian saying to the effect that what doesn't kill you, makes you stronger. And I think that people used to name their kids after these things. Like, 'Raging Horse,' or 'Drought.'"

Sirena didn't know whether or not to laugh.

"They could have named me Drought," said Bullitt, and smiled at her. "I should be thankful."

"I know I am," said Sirena.

Bullitt looked a little weary. "They've done the best they can."

On the way back to Sirena's place, Bullitt swung into another neighborhood in South Central.

"Let's stop here for a minute," said Bullitt. "There's something else I want you to see."

"What?" asked Sirena. She didn't really like surprises and looked around nervously as they drove up to some of the older projects. This was not an area she wanted to be in after dark. "Am I going to like this?"

Bullitt looked at her, as though assessing her. "I think so …"

He pulled up in an empty parking lot and stopped. They got out and walked into a central grassy area surrounded by three-story apartment blocks. "I came here with my Dad when I was little," he said. "My uncle got the contract to install new air conditioning units."

No one was around. It looked completely abandoned. Sirena gripped Bullitt's hand. "Are you sure this is the place?" She could see identical apartment blocks stretching off in either direction.

"I think so," he said again.

They rounded a corner and were facing a huge mural. It had the Mexican flag and the United Farmworkers of America flag and the US flag, all surrounding gigantic portraits of Cesar Chavez, Martin Luther King, and John F. Kennedy. It was painted in the hyper-realist style of the sixties but looked as though it had been neglected for a long time. Parts of it were marked with fresh graffiti.

"Is this it?" whispered Sirena.

Bullitt stood staring up at the mural. "Yeah … isn't it amazing?"

The silence around them was unbroken except for the sound of traffic on the nearby streets. As she glanced around, Sirena could see a couple of plastic Hot Wheels tricycles up on a second-floor lanai. She found this reassuring. Bullitt's face was smooth and serious.

"Great," she said.

"I played with some other kids right here," said Bullitt, his eyes never leaving the mural. "I didn't speak any English yet, but we played anyway. Now that I think about it, I don't know what they were speaking. Later, my Dad told my mother that this place reminded him of home."

A gunning engine punctured the silence. Bullitt seemed to return from a long way away.

"Let's go," he said, and they started back to the car. They could hear voices now, laughing and loud talking in Spanish. But they still saw no one. The sounds bounced around the projects, so you couldn't tell where they came from. They seemed, to Sirena, like ghosts. When she and Bullitt got to the parking lot, there were two cars that hadn't been there before. They got in Bullitt's car and left.

"Do you ever wonder," asked Sirena, "what it would have been like if you had grown up in the Soviet Republic?"

"All the time," said Bullitt, "especially when my parents talk about it. They tell me they came to the U.S. for me, but I wasn't even born yet."

"But they were still thinking about their kids—you—when they came. It couldn't have been easy to leave everything behind."

"I don't know. Probably not. But the way they talk, it wouldn't have been easy to stay."

Bullitt looked at Sirena and appeared to focus on her for the first time since they had left his parents' house. His voice sounded more normal as he spoke.

"When my aunt came, it was just a matter of time before they did, too. When she married my uncle, he sponsored them, guaranteed that they would have jobs."

"Your Mom worked, too?"

"For awhile. Until." He glanced at Sirena, and she nodded.

Sirena was still amazed at Bullitt's background. She had never detected an accent, or if she had, she thought he had grown up in another part of the United States. Los Angeles was full of people who left their homes in Mexico or the midwest or the East as soon as they could and spent the rest of their lives seeking the perfect California lifestyle.

"Maybe you can visit the place they're from someday," said Sirena.

"Yeah. Tuva."

"Tuva? Where is that, exactly?"

"Absolutely in the middle of nowhere. It's where Eastern Europe ends and Mongolia begins. It's so far away that I'm not even sure how you get there." Bullitt was quiet for a minute. "Maybe you fly to Moscow and take a train."

"It sounds like an adventure," Sirena said to Bullitt.

Bullitt smiled. "A job for star children."

Sirena thought of the star-shaped scar on Bullett's back. She had made up a set of stories about star children who would save the universe.

"Is there something there that needs to be fixed? A universe to save?"

"Probably. It's one of those places that doesn't want to be part of the Soviet Republic but doesn't really have a choice. It's a really small country."

"Could you liberate Tuva?"

"Maybe. For about five minutes."

"Well, maybe you could just visit. Assess the situation. What's the worst that could happen?" asked Sirena.

"That I run out of money there and can't come back," said Bullitt.

"You might end up liking it."

"I might," he said. Bullitt pulled the car into the guest parking for Sirena's apartment. "You never know."

He kissed Sirena goodbye before she stepped out of the car.

"What did that word mean?" she asked, stooping to look in at him.

"Which word?"

"What your mother called you when we first got there."

Bullitt's face reddened and he grinned. "It's her pet name for me," he said. "Kadarchy. It means 'little shepherd boy.'"

AQA

There was a place on Second where Sirena wanted to go. Devi had first talked about it in college, tried to get Sirena to take Julio-I-mean-Mike along with whoever Devi was dating at the time.

Julio refused to go.

"Why not?" asked Sirena. "It would be fun."

"Guys would just look at you," he said.

"That's the idea!" said Sirena, brightly. "To see and be seen!"

"Yeah, well, I'd rather be the one seeing you."

Julio was very jealous. He went a lot of places without Sirena in those days. She thought it meant he loved her. She was very young, she thought later.

But now Bullitt wanted to go. "You know that place? The one with the divers from Acapulco and the waterfall? My office is having a party there."

"Is that still around?" asked Sirena. "I thought it closed ages ago."

"Well, I think the owners left, but the divers stayed."

"How's the food?"

"I think it's ironic Mexican, or something."

"Sounds terrible."

"Well, we won't eat anything if it is. Just drink."

"What should I wear?"

"Something very sexy."

"You know I don't do sexy."

"Try," said Bullitt. "Just for me."

Sirena's work clothes were boring, boring, boring. Her casual clothes were cheap, cheap, cheap. Devi, the shopping queen, took her shopping.

"I want to go to the party, too!" Devi loved to go out, was at home in the glittering world.

"It's a party from Bullitt's bank, but I can't imagine they're taking over the whole place, unless it's small."

"It's vast," said Devi. "Rooms within rooms."

"In that case, I'll just go," said Sirena. "Just be there."

Devi dragged Sirena through two shopping malls, flipping through clothes on racks more rapidly than Sirena could keep up. Sirena tried to look at the price tags, but Devi just pushed her hand away. "Not yet," she said. "First we have to find something that would even fit you."

Devi was a size six. Sirena was not.

Finally, they went into a store Sirena had never heard of. Everything was black and white, so that the clothes popped. They were enveloped in some sort of Euro trance music.

A salesperson named Maurice came up to them.

"Help us," said Devi. This was the first time Sirena had ever heard her sound desperate.

"I'll try," he said, looking from one to the other. "What are you looking for?" He bounced slightly to the music. Sirena noticed that he was wearing mascara.

"She has a party at AQA, and her boyfriend wants her to look, you know, hot."

"I am hot," said Sirena, bridling under the scrutiny. "I just don't have party clothes."

"I see," said Maurice. He paused and looked her up and down. "Come with me." He led them to a rack of dresses.

"I almost never wear dresses," said Sirena.

"Just try a couple of things on," said Devi. "Try to be open-minded."

Sirena remembered the fireworks and the ensuing fire. That was the last time she had tried to be open to new experiences.

Sirena went into a dressing room with a curtain that ended about 18" above the floor. She was sure everyone in the mall could see her in her underwear. All the dresses were short and very tight. She opened the curtain while wearing the last one.

"No," she said, as Devi looked at her.

"You're right," she said. "It's not you."

Just then Maurice came up holding out some clothes on hangers.

"Here, try these," he said.

"Leather jeans?" asked Sirena. "White leather jeans?"

"Just put them on," said Devi. "Why not?"

Sirena slithered into the jeans, which actually zipped up. They were surprisingly comfortable once they were on. They had little zippers on the ankles, which she zipped, then unzipped the one to show her tattoo. It took awhile to figure the top out, which was a gauzy turquoise thing. When she got it on, the hem was asymmetrical, coming to a point below her right hip. Sirena looked at herself in the mirror. Then she loosened her hair from its ponytail. When she threw back the curtain, flinging her hair back, hands on hips, they cheered.

Bullitt whistled when he picked her up. "Hot mama," he said. "I'll have to introduce you to the boss while he's still sober."

"Luther won't be there, will he?" asked Sirena.

"You know, I haven't seen Luther for several days. He hasn't been in. In fact, I'm not sure he even works there anymore. No one's talking about it."

Sirena elaborately rearranged the strap to her tiny purse.

"Are you still mad at him?"

"Yes, I'm still mad at him. You don't know what he did."

"Yes, I do, he told me. He figured you had told me, so he apologized."

"He apologized to you? What about me?"

"He said he was sorry. He was just joking around."

Sirena looked at Bullitt. "It wasn't funny."

"I can see that. Look. Personal interaction is not Luther's strong point. You're probably the first woman he's touched since …"

"Since the last time he grabbed someone?"

Bullitt laughed. "Yeah, probably. In any case, I doubt that he was invited tonight."

"Good."

Sirena's cheeks were flush with her anger. Bullitt smiled at her.

"What?"

"You're beautiful," he said.

She almost smiled before putting her hand on his where it rested on the stick shift.

The club had valet parking. The name in neon over the door was a palindrome with all the letters facing the center consonant. The neon was the same color as Frosty Bear. Inside, light was projected in rippling waves, so that everything and everyone looked underwater.

Bullitt's party was in the back corner near the bar, which had the best view of the divers. Every once in awhile, a man—or the one woman—with a perfect body and a tiny bathing suit bottom stepped into a spotlight on a rock platform that jutted out high above the crowd. The music would stop except for a drum roll, and everyone turned to watch. The man leaped out and dove in the shape of a perfect *T* through the giant ferns and palm trees to the artificial lagoon below. There were parrots loose in the trees. Everyone applauded, and the music started again, seemingly more frantic each time. It was lovely. It was steamy. It was loud.

Bullitt's boss was the only one in a suit and tie. He didn't look that much older than they were and didn't appear interested in Sirena at all. He was with a tiny blonde in high heels who didn't look any more comfortable than Sirena felt. Already, two or three empty drinks with little umbrellas surrounded her.

Sirena ordered a mojito, and Bullitt had a beer.

"How exotic," said Sirena at his order.

"You know me, just another guy."

"You know that's not true at all," murmured Sirena, leaning close. She crossed her white leather-clad legs. She felt powerful, seductive, and hoped it wasn't the rum.

As the night wore on, Bullitt drifted away to talk to people. Sirena grew bored and looked around to see if Devi had made it.

A man suddenly leaned up against her shoulder. She turned. It was Bullitt's boss, his tie now loosened. He looked deep into her cleavage.

"I would really, really like to get to know you better," he said, before another man pulled him away.

"Come on, Brad. Let's take a walk."

Sirena thought she glimpsed a woman in an apricot-colored sari flitting across a doorway being pulled by a man's hand.

"Devi?" called Sirena.

Another diver emerged on the platform, the lone spot focused on her as she strode confidently toward the edge. Several people flinched as she approached it. There was a drum roll and a cymbal as the woman flew out in a graceful swan dive, closing her arms above her head in time to knife through the water. After her perfect form had already cut the water, Sirena realized that this time she wasn't wearing a bathing suit at all.

Bullitt had been gone a long time, and Sirena was starting to get hungry. Maybe they could leave and go somewhere with real food.

A figure stumbled out onto the diving ledge, seemingly confused. In the dim rippling light it was impossible to see who it was, but he was wearing street clothes, not one of the divers. People began to murmur and point as the figure stood, swaying drunkenly. The music faltered in confusion then stopped, but the drum roll did not begin.

"Jesus, no!" said someone behind Sirena.

"Don't yell at him. You'll startle him."

The figure peered around like a badger emerging from sleep and began to chuckle. "How the hell do I get down from here?" he asked.

Just then, two men emerged from the fake rock that concealed the door behind him. As they stepped out and grabbed him, the man's shoes seemed to slip on the rock. The two men fell to their knees trying to hold him, but he shot off the ledge feet first. The crowd gasped, and a woman screamed.

There was a tremendous splash at the bottom. The music stopped, and regular lights came on. Everyone looked flat and ordinary as the room was flooded with harsh overhead light. Restaurant personnel gathered around the pool, obscuring their view. People blinked at each other in the glare. Sirena realized that she had a tremendous headache. Soon they could hear sirens, and medics came in with a stretcher. After a long time huddled at the near edge of the pool, the emergency personnel strapped the man onto the stretcher and carried him out. Sirena just got a glimpse of a dripping figure in a white, immobilizing collar. He seemed to be out cold.

"It's Brad," someone said.

Sirena turned. It was Bullitt. "Oh, thank goodness. I was wondering where you were." Sirena hugged him.

"What? You think I'm enough of an idiot to go up there?"

People turned and stared at Bullitt. "It was an accident. He was looking for the men's room," said a woman coldly.

"Oh, sorry. I mean, it's just not something I would do." Bullitt looked around uncomfortably. "Come on. You act like I pushed him, or something. Who was with him, anyway?"

Suddenly, Sirena remembered the earlier encounter. "He was with someone. They came by here."

"Helene?" someone asked.

"No, a man. Brad was really drunk, and he said, 'Come on, Brad, let's take a walk.'"

Brad's date had vanished, and everyone else began to do the same.

"Let's get out of here," said Sirena, and grabbed Bullitt by the hand.

They drove back to Bullitt's place, where they ate Top Ramen and drank beer. Then, very slowly, Bullitt peeled Sirena's white leather jeans off of her, carefully unzipping every zipper right down to her diamond tattoo.

The Accidental Zoo

When Sirena picked him up at LAX, Julio gave her a cool peck on the cheek. He was wearing dark dress slacks and a white shirt, a tie loose around his neck, and the farther they got from the gate, the more uncomfortable he looked.

Sirena had worn a nice dress, but he barely noticed her, distracted by his bags.

"What's in the briefcase?" she asked. "Did they give you homework?"

He glanced down at the case on the floor of the car, reached out, and touched it. "Uh, yes, some draft legislation to go over."

"They expect you to work on your vacation?"

"There's a piece of legislation pending in my area." He looked over at her. "Everybody works all the time."

Sirena pulled out into traffic and headed for Pasadena.

"You should have let me drive," said Julio.

"Oh, sorry," said Sirena. "I forgot. Next time."

Julio hated being a passenger in her car. She wasn't sure if he was like this with everyone. Probably only with girls.

Julio picked up his briefcase and opened it on his lap.

"So, how are you?" she asked.

He glanced up. "Fine. Busy."

"So I see." This was not going to be an easy visit. Sirena wondered now what had possessed her to call his mother and offer to pick him up. She felt her throat beginning to ache in that familiar way.

"I'm sorry, baby. It's just that I've got a lot to do. Bill really wanted me to stick around awhile longer."

"Bill?"

"Congressman MacIntosh."

"Oh. He wanted you to miss Christmas with your family?"

"No. Just stay another day to finish this up. It goes into subcommittee when session resumes."

"Isn't he coming home? Or does his family live out there?"

"He's coming back tomorrow. I'm supposed to call him on Friday."

Sirena drummed her fingers on the steering wheel. A necklace of red lights stretched out before them.

"I was hoping to go somewhere."

"Oh? Well, go ahead. Don't let me stop you."

"No. I was hoping to take you with me. To Tijuana."

"What? Why?"

"There's a place I want to visit."

"No, man, I don't want to cross the border. It takes too fucking long."

Sirena could hear his composure slipping, and his carefully constructed accent with it. She said nothing, only drove.

"Okay. What place?"

"You're too busy. I can see. I'll just have to go with Devi. Just two girls alone in Tijuana." Her voice was teasing.

"I don't think that's a good idea. Something might happen."

"Something might!"

"Sirena, c'mon now. That's nothing to joke about. Bodies turn up everyday. You should see some of the information about crime on the border that comes across my desk. Things the public doesn't hear about."

"Julio, relax. We go to the beach at Rosario all the time. There's a new zoo in Tijuana I want to visit."

He shut his briefcase. "Call me Mike," said Julio.

This was a change he had made when he moved to Washington, D.C.

"Mike."

"There's a perfectly good zoo in San Diego," he said. "Why can't you go there?"

"This is a special one. It started by accident. As a refuge for animals that got left at the border."

"They can't even take care of the people there. Why start an animal refuge?"

"It's animals they've taken from smugglers," said Sirena. "Parrots and snakes and other stuff. Circus animals. You'd be surprised!"

"Nothing would surprise me."

They drove on in silence.

At Julio's house his family spilled out the door to meet him. His mother's hair was freshly done, and his youngest brother and sister plastered themselves to his pant legs.

"Lookin' sharp, dude!" said his father, rising from the couch where he had been watching television. His father was on disability, but his mother sold real estate. She had helped Sirena get her job in Sonny's office. Julio and his father shook hands, then embraced.

"Papa," said Julio.

"Julio, my man."

"Come in, come in," said his mother to Sirena. "Don't stand out there like a stranger."

"Thanks," said Sirena, stepping in the door.

"My goodness, you are more beautiful than ever. Isn't she beautiful, honey?" she said to her husband.

"Of course, almost as beautiful as you."

The younger children giggled as Sirena crouched down in her short skirt to give them hugs.

"We miss you," said Mimi.

"Well, I miss you!" said Sirena.

"Why don't you visit anymore?"

"Oh, I don't know. I should, huh?"

"Déja la," said Julio's mother. "She works now. No time for play. Are they giving you any time off?"

"Well, today I left early to get Jul—I mean, Mike. I was going to take Friday off, too."

"Can you stay for dinner?"

Sirena looked at Julio to see if there was any encouragement. He was watching football with his father.

"Oh, don't mind them. Stay and talk to me, at least. I want to hear about your mom and dad, and you, of course."

"All right," said Sirena. She sat down with Malibu Barbie and Ken in her lap, as Mimi began an elaborate story about a party to which they were going. Greg, the youngest, lay flat on his stomach, making zooming noises as he ran his Matchbox cars up to, and finally over, Julio's dress shoes.

"Quit it!" said Julio, pulling his feet back.

"Watch his shoes!" said his father. "Do you have to do that right here?"

Greg sat up, hurt and confused.

"Come on, Greg, let's see your cars," said Sirena. The boy got reluctantly to his feet and went over to sit by Sirena.

Julio's mother came in with drinks. "Why don't you relax, mijo?" she said to Julio. "Put on some regular clothes?"

"These are regular clothes," he said. But he stood up, and said to Sirena, holding up his hand, "Prestame your car keys."

She reached into her handbag and tossed them, and Julio stepped over the younger children to retrieve his luggage from the trunk.

While they were eating, Julio's brother Raúl came slamming in the door and went straight past the dining room.

"Raúl!" called his father. "Raúl, come here."

They could hear the toilet flush.

"Just a second, man," said Raúl as he slouched in. "I had to pee!"

"Please don't talk like that in front of the younger children," said his mother. "Besides, we have a guest!"

"Hey, Sirena," he said.

"Hey, Raúl," she answered.

"Say hello to your brother," said his father.

"Bro—'" said Raúl, and gave Julio a complicated handshake.

"Where have you been?" said his mother. "You knew Mike was due home today."

"Who? Oh, yeah," said Raúl. He sat at the table and helped himself to some food. "Mr. Mike González."

"That's his choice," said his father.

"Excuse me," said Julio after dinner. "I've got to check on something."

He retreated to his parents' bedroom, and they could hear him on the phone.

"What time is it in Washington?" asked his mother.

"Maybe … eleven o'clock?" said Sirena.

"That's late," said Mimi.

"Yeah, that's way past my bedtime!" said Greg.

"Go do your homework," said his mother.

"But I don't have any!"

"Well then, take your plate in the kitchen."

"I guess I better go now," said Sirena. "It takes awhile to get back."

"When will we see you?"

"I don't know. I'm working tomorrow. It's up to Julio, I guess." Sirena tried to keep her expression neutral. "Thanks for dinner." She helped Greg and Mimi clear the table and went outside.

"Come say goodbye to your girlfriend!" she could hear his mother yell. She knew it was not for her benefit.

Julio came out and stood by her car. She opened the passenger door and handed him his briefcase.

"You don't want to forget this!" she said.

"Thanks. No, I don't."

They stood awkwardly in the dim light from the porch.

"Well, let me know if you want to go on Friday," said Sirena.

"Still fixed on that, huh?"

Sirena didn't know what to do. He had been like an iceburg all evening. She knew she would cry if she tried to say anything, so she went around and got in the car instead.

"I'll call you," he mouthed through the windshield, then turned and went into the house.

At work the next day, Gloria, the front office person, said, "Well?"

Sirena shrugged and tried to smile. "We might get together tomorrow."

"That sounds promising," said Gloria.

Sirena went through the motions, adding addresses to the company's database, purging others. It was quiet, peaceful in the office, with many of the realtors taking a long weekend. Sonny had left the day before to visit his parents in Indiana. The agents' photos, framed in red and green plaid and trimmed with white cotton wool and glitter, decorated the display board that faced the street. "Happy Holidays from your Friendly Realtors," it said at the bottom. "Friendly Realtors" was the name of the agency. Gloria had put the display together. She had tried to get Sirena to have her picture included, but she had declined.

"I don't sell real estate," she had said. "The focus should be on the agents."

"But you're a part of this office!" said Gloria.

"I know," said Sirena. "But they should get the attention. And you, too! Since you deal with the public." Sirena knew that Gloria wanted to include her own photo.

"Well, all right," said Gloria. "Suit yourself."

Friday morning, Julio still hadn't called. Sirena was packing her car in a desultory manner when the phone rang.

"Hello?"

"It's me."

"And?"

"Do you still want to go?"

"Well, like I said, I'm going. In fact, you almost missed me."

"What about Devi?"

"She couldn't make it." In fact, Sirena had not even mentioned it to her. If Julio had decided to go, she wanted to be alone with him.

"And you were planning to go by yourself?"

"Sure. Why not?" Sirena could feel Julio's agitation on the telephone.

"Well, why don't you pick me up on the way?"

"Okay. I'll see you then."

Sirena let him drive to Tijuana. He was wearing jeans today, and one of his old shirts.

"Did you call your boss?"

"Bill? Yeah."

"So everything is worked out?"

"I'll have plenty to do when I get back tonight."

"You could have brought it in the car. I could have driven."

Julio shrugged. "It's okay."

The traffic slowed as they approached the border. This time of year there was even more traffic than usual, especially going south, as people returned to see their families for the holidays. For some, this was the only time they got home. Children selling baskets and balloon vendors began to appear and walk along the cars as they sorted themselves into lanes to cross.

A guard signaled for them to slow, then motioned for them to go ahead as he glanced in the car. At the crossing a woman asked them where they were headed.

"Tijuana," said Julio.

"Got insurance?" she asked.

"Yes," said Sirena, pointing to the sticker in the window.

They showed their ID and crossed.

The streets were thick now, and Julio had to struggle to stay in the traffic going downtown. "Where now?" he asked.

"Parque Morelos," said Sirena. "Just follow the signs."

"You been here before?"

"No. A woman in my office told me about it." Sirena opened her purse. "She gave me this brochure to use today from an animal protection group that's giving money to it. It has directions and an address if we get lost."

"Right."

"Well, we can always ask."

A forest of signs appeared on a busy corner, and they slowed to see if Parque Morelos was listed. A car, then another honked behind them.

"The fog is burning off," said Sirena. "It should be a nice day."

"I'm hungry," said Julio.

"Let's find a lot by the park, then look for some place to eat."

They followed more signs, then little boys motioning to park the car. Julio gave one of them a dollar as they locked up.

"Five dollars," said the boy. "Five dollars to park."

They looked around. "There's a place to put money," said Sirena.

"No, no, five dollars to me," said the boy. He looked about eleven years old.

"One dollar now," said Sirena. "And four when we come back, and the car looks nice."

"Okay," said the boy. "I wash it for you." He whipped a grimy rag from his back pocket and began polishing the bumper.

"Think you'll ever see your car again?" said Julio.

"I hope so."

As they walked along the perimeter of the park, Julio seemed to relax a little. He held his arms more loosely and began to take longer strides.

"I'm sorry you work so hard," said Sirena.

"Yeah, but it's exciting. It's hard to describe what it's like to be at the center of things."

A man tried to sell them a balloon, but they declined. They passed shoeshine boys and a man wearing a stack of sombreros six feet high.

"I haven't been here in a long time," said Julio. "Since that time we all drove to El Bufo."

"That's right," said Sirena. "And my brother spilled a Coke all over that cowboy's shirt. Boy, was he mad."

"I thought we were all going to prison that night," said Julio. "I was scared, man."

Sirena remembered how reluctant Julio had been to go to Mexico even then. "How come you don't like Mexico ...?" she started to say "Julio," then closed her mouth on it.

"I don't know. It's okay. I just don't like—trouble." He sighed. "Everything is complicated here."

They passed an American sailor sitting on a park bench necking with a Mexican girl. Sirena was reminded of the Paul Simon song about lovers on a bench.

"There it is," she said, pointing. A sign said, "Zoo." "Let's get something to eat and come back."

They found a sidewalk café and ordered lunch. Sirena ordered taquitos, and Julio had huevos rancheros.

"How is it?" she asked. Sirena could see that he was relishing the food.

"We don't have anything like this in D.C.," he said. "Truthfully, the food isn't much there. And the coffee is worse." He chewed some more. "Sometimes we get up to the Adams Morgan district, but it's more like, you know, Cuban food."

Are you seeing someone? Sirena wanted to ask, but was not sure she wanted to know the answer. Ever since her dream, in which she saw him from an aerial view telling lies to someone, she was sure that he was. She must have known it in her heart all along, but her head would not see it until she dreamed it.

"What's your apartment like?" she asked instead.

He nodded, his mouth full. "It's okay. You know. It'll do. I'm hardly ever in it."

She watched how his hair fell over his forehead, how his lips were full without being coarse.

"What are you looking at?" he said, smiling briefly, embarrassed.

"You," said Sirena. "I haven't seen you in six months."

"Yeah, I guess it has been awhile. Sorry I've been so busy. It's really hard being so far away."

"Yes, it is."

"You know I asked you to come with me," he said.

"I know," said Sirena. "It's not your fault. I just don't think there's a place for me there." She didn't say, "But you didn't ask me to marry you."

"So what do you do all day? At work? That's so exciting?"

Julio looked down again, flushed. "You wouldn't understand."

"Try me," said Sirena, softly.

"We set policy. We answer constituents' questions and help with their problems. We write legislation that will affect the way everyone lives in the whole country," he said, as though reciting a holy creed.

"And why wouldn't I understand that?" asked Sirena.

"I don't know, baby. It's just so different from here."

"From Tijuana? Where do you think your constituents are from, anyway?"

"You know what I mean. It's different outside the Beltway."

Julio finished his lunch and stood up. Sirena put a couple of dollars on the table.

"I'll get it," he said.

"That's just the tip." Sirena went to use the bathroom, and when she returned, Julio stood on the sidewalk, watching the traffic.

At the zoo they paid their entrada of ten pesos. Cages appeared to be randomly scattered along some gravel paths. There was a cage full of tiny green parrots and another of monkeys that were sitting high up by the top. They were trying to escape the attention of a noisy group of children with their faces pressed against the mesh below them. "¡Changos!" they shouted. "¡Changitos!"

The biggest crowd was around a lion.

"Nala," Sirena read off of the corner. "I read about her."

Nala lay in the dusty shade, her tail flicking at the persistent flies. Next to her enclosure was a tiger. It was more restless and paced back and forth obsessively. Julio stood and looked at it silently. It, too, ignored the crowd, looking right through them as though intent on an appointment with a specific person, one who had not yet shown up. It let out a groan, and the children giggled nervously.

"I hear you, brother," said Julio.

Sirena moved on to where an albino anaconda was draped across some bare branches in a cage. It had been confiscated from an exotic dancer in one of the local clubs. You had to look hard to see it, so translucent was its skin in the shade of a tarp that partially covered the cage. It reminded her of a children's rosary she had once seen. It had been made out of plastic and glowed in the dark and had come in a clear plastic egg. She was staring at the snake so hard that, when it finally shifted, she could see an after-image of its former position, as though there were now two snakes instead of one.

Julio walked up beside her, where she stood in contemplation of the apparition.

"So when did you get interested in animal rights?"

Sirena glanced at him. "Always, I think." She turned back to the snake. "Since I was little. I used to rescue birds from our cat."

"You going to start burning down research labs? Throwing paint on ladies in fur coats?"

"Do I look like someone who throws paint on people?" said Sirena. "You know, my mom used to have a fur coat. Kind of a little cape. I wonder if she still has it."

"If she does, you could take it outside and burn it."

Sirena refused to take the bait. "The moths probably ate it."

At the end of the row was a cage that appeared to be empty. A mother and her child stood peering inside.

"¿Qué hay adentro?" asked Sirena.

"Una zarigüeya," said the mother, and pointed. A dim shape lay gently breathing in the corner, partially burrowed into some sawdust. As she stared at it, Sirena could make out the rat-like tail of an opossum.

"Esta dormido," whispered the child, and put her finger to her pouted lips. There was a ring of pink cotton candy around her mouth.

Sirena nodded and put her finger to her own lips. After a moment she turned away to where Julio stood looking off into the distance. She wondered if he missed smoking, something he had given up a couple of years ago. He looked older where he stood in the sun now, fine wrinkles beginning to show around his eyes.

"Seen enough?" he asked, stepping back.

"Yeah, but I'm going to give them a donation."

"There's a box," said Julio, pointing to the battered wooden box with a padlock attached to the front of a small information kiosk. "Help yourself."

Sirena took out a twenty and folded it, making sure that the corner got all the way in the slot. In the time that it took to open her wallet, a constellation of children clustered around her.

"Chiclets," said one. "Un dollar."

Sirena distributed a couple of dimes and quarters and they made their escape.

"We better go," said Julio. "The traffic is going to be bad."

Sirena stepped close to him, and he draped his arm casually, unconsciously, around her shoulders. She leaned into him, smelling the newness of his shirt and the slightly salty smell of his body.

He seemed to notice her for the first time, and his indifferent hand suddenly tightened on her shoulder. Sirena looked into his eyes and saw a coldness she did not recognize. His hand tightened to a painful grip, and he kissed her hard, ostentatiously. As she struggled to pull away, he held her fast, his mouth fastened upon hers. Then he released her, and she almost fell. As she regained her footing, Sirena saw that people were staring. She felt bruised, violated.

Whatever he had felt for her before, she thought, had turned to this.

Sirena wiped her mouth and walked away from him, toward the car. She did not care if he followed her or not. Her vision—of the trees, the people, the bright balloons—was blurred with tears and anger.

She did not look back to see if he was following, but Sirena knew he was too chicken to stay behind by himself.

When they reached the car, the boy they'd left it with was nowhere to be seen.

"Where's my guardian angel?" Sirena cried out.

Just as they pulled away, he came running up.

"Five dollar! Five dollar!" he screamed, pounding on the hood of the car.

"Let's just go," said Julio, sounding nervous.

"Wait," commanded Sirena. She rolled down her window and handed him a five. "Gracias," she said.

"De nada," he answered, and waved them on with the air of a military leader.

"I thought you only promised him four more," said Julio.

"Shall we go back and ask him for change?" asked Sirena. "Besides, the car is fine. It was still cheaper than we would have paid at the San Diego Zoo."

The crossing north was fairly easy. Sirena noted that, each time she crossed, the immigration police would ask "What country were you born in?"

"It's just to make you say, 'United States,'" she had told Devi. "They want to hear if you say, 'Joonited Estates.'

"And if you do?" Devi had asked.

"Then they take your car apart and look for drugs."

Sirena smiled at the memory, then looked over at Julio. They had not spoken since getting in the car. She looked at his hands and remembered when he could not keep them off of her.

At the house Sirena pulled into the driveway and put the car in park. She did not turn off the engine.

There had once been a time when things made sense, when she could see into the future clearly. But ever since Julio had finished law school then moved to Washington, D.C., Sirena was not sure what she wanted. The poor truth was that, Julio/Mike no longer wanted her. She didn't think she liked what he had become either, but she couldn't get him out of her head, or her heart, to make room for someone else.

Julio sighed. "I'll call you tomorrow. Okay?"

"Why?" she whispered, a sudden rush of tears obscuring her voice.

"Well, just because. Don't cry, baby."

"I don't want to," she said, hoarsely.

Backing out of the driveway, Sirena almost hit a speeding SUV that honked as it zoomed by. Turning back, Sirena glimpsed Julio's mother looking out the window of the house, waving, but she did not wave back.

That's it, thought Sirena. I'll never show him my feelings again.

She thought of the albino snake—mysterious, forlorn—draped like a magic necklace across its branch. As she merged into the late afternoon traffic going north, Sirena wondered if the snake remembered its previous life, if it had left a mate behind somewhere in the jungle. Did snakes keep the same mate? Obviously not, thought Sirena as she slammed the car into fourth gear.

Wherever her gaze rested on the way home, she saw Julio's black hair falling over his forehead as he bent toward her, the memory of that kiss aleady beginning to cloud the memory of other kisses she had worked so hard to keep.

Do You Know the Way to the Monkey House?

One night after work Sirena met Bullitt at Lucky John's for pizza.

"What do you want to do? A movie?"

"I don't know," she said. Since her trip to Tijuana with Julio-call-me-Mike, she had been subdued. It didn't matter, she kept telling herself. She had known she would lose him as soon as he moved to the East Coast.

"Still brooding about Julio?" asked Bullitt.

"I guess so," she said. She had told him the rudiments of the adventure. "I'm not sure why I'm still upset."

"Probably because you didn't have a say in the matter," said Bullitt. "It's always more pleasant to be the dumper than the dumpee."

"Yeah," said Sirena. "Thanks. That makes me feel much better."

"I know something that will cheer you up."

"An execution?" asked Sirena. "Baby torture?"

"Better than that. I want to take you to a place you haven't been before."

"Hmmm," said Sirena, toying with her chocolate milkshake. "Does this involve futbol?"

"No, not that I know of," said Bullitt. "Although my father asks about you all the time. He was quite smitten by you."

"Oh, well, that's nice. At least someone is."

"Sirena," said Bullitt, taking her hands in his and trying to look into her downcast eyes. "You know how I feel."

"I do?" she asked, looking up.

"Come on," said Bullitt, standing up. "Let's check this place out."

They got in the car and drove north up to Laurel Canyon. Two miles into the hills, they were surrounded by trees and shrubbery.

"It's like a little jungle up here," said Sirena. "One minute you're in the city, the next you're far away."

Bullitt slowed the car at a side street. "I think it's up here," he said, turning.

The street narrowed, and they passed a No Outlet sign. Beyond that, the road turned to dirt. The houses here were invisible behind barriers of trees and oleanders run wild.

"Are you sure this is the way?" asked Sirena. "Where are we going, anyway?"

"Trust me," said Bullitt. "I got careful directions from a friend."

Bullitt had not consulted notes or a map the entire time. Sirena had noticed before that Bullitt could remember a lot of things that she could not.

They came to a neon yellow plastic ribbon that marked a dirt track.

"This is it," he said, and pulled the car into a gap in the weeds. A homemade private property, No Trespassing sign leaned dangerously over an embankment above them. Sirena squirmed nervously in her seat. Some of these places had armed private guards, she had heard. Reasons to keep people out. Celebrities. Drugs. The vices that, even in L.A., needed to be kept secret.

The track leveled out, and Sirena thought she could glimpse some walls or buildings ahead.

Although it was nearly dark, Bullitt kept the headlights off. As they rounded a bend, Sirena could hear odd, high-pitched sounds.

"What is this?" she asked.

"You'll see."

They pulled into an open area from which they could see a pink hacienda-style mansion with a red tile roof. Bullitt turned off the engine, and Sirena leaned forward, straining to see more detail. A light was on inside, and she could make out a moving figure now and then.

"Is this a party?" she asked, placing her hand on the door.

"Wait," said Bullitt, putting his hand on her arm without looking away from the house. "Don't get out just yet."

One of the figures came closer, and as her eyes began to adjust to the darkness, Sirena could see that it was some kind of animal. It sat up, regarding them.

"Why, it's a monkey!" she said, delighted.

The monkey opened its mouth and let out a shrill scream, and what seemed like hundreds of monkeys came toward them out of the bushes, the building, and the surrounding trees.

"Lock the doors," said Bullitt.

The car was swarmed by screeching monkeys that tried to open the doors, fingered the antennas and wipers, clambered on the hood and roof of the car, and bared their teeth in the windshield. When it was clear that Bullitt and Sirena were not coming out, a few began to lose interest, then more and more dropped off and sauntered back to the main building.

"Wow," said Sirena, stunned. She could now see the dilapidated condition of the building, the hanging, shredded screens, the broken windows. Still, there was a light on inside.

"Does someone live here?" she asked.

She and Bullitt had been gripping each other's arms all this time. Now he relaxed.

"I don't know," he said. "Someone at work told me about it. People come up here and feed them."

"We don't have any food."

"I know. I forgot."

Sirena could see that it had once been a beautiful place with a courtyard off to the right flanked by shaggy palm trees. Now this, too, was overrun with monkeys, all the same kind, scratching, eating, screaming in each other's faces.

"I can't believe no one takes care of them," she said. "Even if they didn't, the city or the county couldn't just leave them here."

"Maybe they'll take over the city," said Bullitt.

"Maybe they already have."

Bullitt laughed. "That would explain a lot."

As night fell, it became more and more difficult to see. Once in a while, one of the monkeys came back to the car as though checking to see if they had changed their minds about getting out or distributing some food.

"I can't believe all this," said Sirena. "I wonder if this used to belong to some famous actress. It looks abandoned, but then there's that light."

"Maybe monkeys like light, too."

"Then someone's paying the electric bill for them. I'm going to check it out." She started to open her door.

"I don't think that's a good idea," said Bullitt. "They look like they could be dangerous."

"I just want to go close enough to look in the window, see where the light is coming from. Maybe there's someone in there."

"Then I'll go with you," said Bullitt, without much conviction.

"Why? We'll just make more noise."

Sirena cracked her car door. None of the monkeys seemed to notice. She carefully climbed out, then crouched down, her fingertips touching the cracked cement. Slowly, she made her way closer to the window, where she could now see the remnants of jagged bamboo blinds hanging in one corner, the light from inside coming through them.

A low, crumbling wall separated the driveway from the courtyard. Rather than trying to open the rusted gate, Sirena leaned out over the wall, trying to see into the window beyond the blinds.

Just then, a sentinel's shriek pierced the air as a monkey that had been strolling the veranda spotted her. Sirena raced for the car as the monkey hordes descended. She slammed the door, leaving a few ends of her hair outside that were promptly snatched out by the enraged monkeys.

"Ow! Ow! Ow!" she said, pulling her hair away from them.

The monkeys pressed their faces to the glass, demon-like now in the dark, howling their fury at the two of them. Their tiny hands were like dark starfish on the windshield, constantly moving as the monkeys searched for a way in—any weakness, any latch that would twist or pull out.

"They're really cussing you now," said Bullitt.

Sirena sat heaving, her eyes glittering with adrenaline. The monkeys' screams began to turn piteous, as though they were begging now.

"Well?" asked Bullitt.

"Well, what?"

"Did you see anything?"

"Sort of," said Sirena. She was putting her hair into a ponytail, rubbing her scalp where the hair had been plucked out.

"You know that scene in *Psycho* ..." she continued.

"Yes? Which one? The shower scene?"

"No. The one where Norman Bates is talking to his mother, and you just see her in her chair from the back ..."

"You saw someone sitting in a chair?"

"I think so. By the light. There's a lamp in there. And a big chair with its back to the window, and there seems to be someone, or something, in it."

"Alive?"

"I couldn't tell. I just got a glimpse."

Bullitt stared at her.

"You want to go look yourself?"

The monkeys' screams had not stopped. Those on the windshield peered intently in at them, looking from Bullitt's eyes to Sirena's and back again, like customers who have been bilked by a salesman, demanding satisfaction. Apparently, someone getting out of the car was too much of a provocation, and their frenzy echoed off the surrounding hills.

"Let's go," said Bullitt, starting the car.

The monkeys clinging to the hood immediately jumped off but did not let up their cries.

As Bullitt and Sirena reached the end of the drive, he turned on his lights, only to find that they were almost on top of another car. Bullitt hit the brakes, and after a moment, the other car backed up to a wider spot, allowing them to pass. As they drew alongside, the driver rolled down his window and leaned out. Bullitt opened his window.

"Do you know the way to the monkey house?" asked the driver.

From here, the sound was fainter, a constant chatter, with louder outbursts. It could have been peacocks or some other exotic noise.

"Yeah," said Bullitt. "Up there on the left."

Later that night they tried to make love, but their bodies felt large and awkward, their hands too clumsy and wide to express anything they might have felt for each other. They put their arms around each other and lay in the silence that fell between them.

Sinners Find Rest in Gehenna

The call was on Sirena's answering machine when she returned from work on Friday. She recognized the voice of Bullitt's father—the heavy consonants, the care taken to be understood. He called her "Miss." His voice was thick with grief.

The river was flooding, he said. The Los Angeles River, usually nonexistent, was flooding. During the storm, the car must have skidded out of control and into the viaduct. Sirena imagined the acres of cement that they passed over everyday. How tempting it was, sometimes, to think about swerving out of traffic and cutting down the steep embankment, surging ahead of everyone the way they did in the movies. Down in the cool, smooth cement channels where people probably lived or did things best hidden from the rest of us.

They had found Bullitt's car, but not Bullitt. Instead, there was the body of a young woman strapped into the passenger seat. It was unclear whether or not Bullitt had even been in the car. They were still looking for him. Had she heard from him?

Sirena immediately called Bullitt's place and got no answer. Then she called his parents. His father answered the phone brusquely.

"This is Sirena," she said. "Bullitt's friend."

"Have you heard from him?" he asked, anxiously.

"Not for a couple of days. When was the last time you heard from him?"

"Last weekend. He came to help his mother put up curtains. He seemed fine then," he added, as though impending tragedy would have been apparent.

"Have you called his friends? Maybe he loaned his car to someone."

"We called the bank. He did not go to work on Friday."

"I'll let you know if I hear from him," said Sirena. "Maybe he'll call."

"Okay," said his father. "I am waiting to hear back from police."

Sirena tried to think of something comforting to say. "I'm sure he is okay."

"Yes," he said. "Thank you."

She called Devi, but she also did not answer. Sirena stayed in that night in hopes that Bullitt would call. She watched the news programs with their helicopters and reporters standing out in the rain by the latest wreck. One showed Bullitt's car, dented and twisted, as it was pulled from the viaduct. Her stomach lurched, and she turned off the television before calling his number again.

When Sirena awoke the next morning, it took her a minute to remember what had happened. The radio alarm clock continued to report damage and injury from the storm. Over three inches had fallen in less than twenty-four hours. Her limbs felt leaden, and she rose slowly and pulled on sweats to wear until she could get a cup of coffee into her system. She had left a message—two messages—on Bullitt's phone the previous night, hoping he had let someone borrow his car, hoping he would call. Bullitt was always so good at explanations.

At eight a.m. the phone rang.

"Is this Sirena?" the voice asked.

"Yes!" Sirena almost shouted.

"This is Assumpta, Devi's cousin. We met once."

"Yes," said Sirena. "I remember. Hello."

"Hello. Listen, something terrible has happened."

"What?" asked Sirena. "What?"

"There was a terrible accident yesterday."

Sirena sat down. "What happened?" she whispered.

"Devi was in an automobile accident. She was a passenger in someone else's car, and the driver apparently lost control of the car during the storm. But the driver has not been located, and they do not know whether he survived."

"And Devi?"

The cousin hesitated. "She did not survive."

"No," whispered Sirena. She could not say more.

Devi's father got on the phone. "The car is registered to someone named Bullitt Tagrib. Did you know him?"

Sirena's voice would not obey her. A chill swept over her, a numbness that she could not control. Her mind was racing.

"Hello?" said Mr. Parekh. "Are you there?"

"Yes," said Sirena. "I knew him. But I did not know that they knew each other."

"Who is this Bullitt fellow?" he asked. "Devi is normally at work on Friday morning. Did they work together?"

"Bullitt worked for a bank. He was a teller."

"He is missing," said Sirena.

"Yes, I know," said Mr. Parekh.

Sirena promised to come over as soon as she was dressed. Sirena wondered whether or not to call her parents. She decided she had better, in case they were worried about her and tried to call while she was gone.

A few minutes later the phone rang again. The police wanted to send a detective around to interview her. She told them she was on her way to Devi's parents but would wait for them.

After she hung up, Sirena panicked. Did she need a lawyer? Should she call someone to be with her while the police were there? Sirena did not trust the police. There were too many stories. She changed quickly into jeans and a sweater, but a detective was on the intercom within ten minutes, leaving her little choice but to let him come up. He brought Sirena's newspaper in with him from the hall. In large type, it blared the headline: *Record Rains Cause Massive Damage—One Dead, Three Missing and Presumed Drowned.*

Officer Hunicutt introduced himself and showed his badge, which Sirena pretended to inspect. She offered him a seat on the couch and sat across the coffee table from him. He left heavy, wet footprints on her beige carpet. It was still raining outside.

"Were there others in the car?" she asked anxiously, scanning the news articles.

"No, ma'am. Those were in other accidents. But those are just the people who have been reported. We're still getting accident reports from all over."

"Bullitt Tagrib's parents told us you are a friend or girlfriend to Mr. Tagrib. Is that right?"

"Yes. Friend. Maybe girlfriend."

"When was the last time you spoke with him?"

"Maybe … Wednesday."

"Did he say anything about leaving town?"

"No …"

"No change in his behavior or buying habits, like, say, a new car? Some other big purchase?"

"No …" Sirena was puzzled. "You found his car, right? Isn't it the silver Honda?"

The officer sighed. "Yes, ma'am. But there seem to be some irregularities at his place of employment as well. We were hoping you might have some information for us."

"The bank?" asked Sirena. "He almost never talks about his job. Sometimes he tells funny stories about the customers, like the woman with the matching black scotty dogs or the retired gentleman who withdraws fifty dollars from the bank every Friday to 'take his sweetie out on the town.'"

"How about Ms. Parekh. Were you acquainted with her?"

"Yes, very well. We went to college together. I've known her longer than Bullitt. But I didn't realize they knew each other. This whole thing is really strange. It's really awful."

The officer shifted as though he found that significant. "You'd be surprised the things people keep secret," he said, shaking his head like he could tell her stories.

"Did Mr. Tagrib have a habit of loaning his car to people? Like, did you ever borrow it?"

"No, I have a car. I never drove his car."

"Did you know his other friends?"

Sirena had to think. "No. I first met him at the movies in Venice Beach. There are other people who also go all the time, and we say hi, but I'm not sure if he knows them any better than I do. He always sits with me if we are both there."

Officer Hunicutt took down the name of the movie theater.

"Have you been to his apartment?"

"Yes."

"Do you have a key to it?"

"No."

"Do you know if anyone else had access to the apartment?"

Sirena frowned. "Maybe his parents. Maybe … I don't know." She shook her head, smiling.

"Is there something you would like to tell us about that?"

"It's just—he used to tell these stories. It was just a joke. About how other people live in our apartments and houses when we are out. Because it's so hard to find a place to live in LA."

The officer wrote earnestly.

Sirena looked at her work shoes kicked off by the door from the day before.

"Is there any place he might be right now that you know of, a favorite place, a weekend getaway?"

"Not that I know of. The only place I ever went with him was the movies, here, his place, and once to his parents. Sometimes we went out to eat, but no place special."

"Any place he talked about visiting?"

"No. Well, Tuva once."

"Tuva?"

"It's where his parents are from. It's in Eastern Europe, Mongolia. It's not the sort of place you just go."

The officer paused. "How do you spell that?"

"T, u, v, a."

He wrote slowly, carefully.

"Well, thank you, Miss. I guess that's all for now." He handed her his card. "Give me a call if you hear from him or think of anything. Sometimes people panic or go into shock, then show up later."

"I will," said Sirena. She still could not believe this was happening. Surely, it was all a joke, a bad dream, one of Bullitt's elaborate ruses that had gotten completely out of hand. Maybe he and Devi were conspiring to scare her. Maybe it hadn't really been Devi in the car after all. But someone, whether she knew who it was or not, was dead.

Sirena felt a sudden wave of jealousy sweep through her, immediately followed by guilt. She poured another cup of coffee and wondered if she could get to Pasadena in the rain. She called her parents.

"Where are you?" said her mother.

"At home, but something has happened. I need to go to Devi's parents' house."

"Why?"

"Something has happened to Devi. She was in a car accident."

"I don't think you should go out. Some people have died. Did you know that?"

Sirena felt her throat catch. She couldn't say it. "Yes," she whispered. "I'll call you later. Okay? Bye." Sirena hung up quickly, unable to continue talking.

Traffic was bad on all the freeways with police cars directing people away from the worst of the flooding. Sirena strained her eyes in the grey mist that rose from the pavement, trying to see the orange cones that funneled cars, blocked drains and low areas. The radio was on, but she could not concentrate on the traffic warnings and street closures, so she followed the route she remembered driving with Devi to her parents' house.

When Sirena got to Pasadena, she drove slowly through the flooded intersections. Several cars were parked on the street outside of the white, ranch-style house with bright yellow shutters.

Sirena parked down the block and sat in the car for a moment, watching the rain. She had never felt so alone, even when her former boyfriend, Julio, had moved to the East Coast a year earlier.

Where was Bullitt? Sirena was sure he wasn't dead. Was that policeman saying they thought Bullitt had robbed the bank? She thought of how she and Bullitt used to make up stories about the star children, how they would gather one day on a planet they pronounced as a sneeze. That his scar marked him as one of the children destined to save the universe. She and Bullitt had told each other this story for so long that it seemed more real than the ugly little crime he had first described, the attack and robbery of his pregnant mother that was the source of the scar on his back.

Sirena thought of Bullitt's mother the way she had first seen her—kneeling in her vegetable garden, digging with a spoon. Of course, she had to have a scar—not only the one on her body, but the enduring grief of coming so close to losing her child, of having a child under such circumstances. And now this.

She remembered Bullitt spread out on his coffee table, surrounded by Pez dispensers like an Egyptian mummy lying in state. He had seemed especially strange that day. What did Sirena really know about Bullitt? Or his family? She only met his parents the one time.

She prayed in her way, sitting there in her car in the rain with Devi's family waiting inside. Sirena prayed that Bullitt would come back, that it was all a misunderstanding, that he had loaned his car to Devi or a mutual friend of theirs, that he had been home all along, asleep, and safe. That someone else had Devi's ID. Maybe both were stolen—Bullitt's car and Devi's ID—by a band of criminals. She prayed that they were both safe somehow in a place closer than Gehenna. She would even forgive them for seeing each other behind her back, planning an adventure without her, if only, dear God, they would turn up safe.

Sirena heard a noise down the street and looked out the windshield of her car. It was streaming with rain. She flicked the windshield wipers once.

In that moment of clearing, she saw a golden desert drenched in light. Coming toward her were two people on a camel—Bullitt in an Arab-style headdress and Devi in a sari. Devi, riding behind Bullitt, carried a parasol with golden fringe to shield herself from the sun. Around her neck was the albino snake from the zoo in Tijuana, and Sirena understood that the snake and Devi were dead. Bullitt's face was unreadable, his eyes shaded by the headdress from the strong light. She could not tell if he was dead or alive.

The windshield wiper descended, and the scene disappeared. Sirena flicked the wiper again but saw only wet, shiny pavement, the cars lining the curb, the perfect neighborhood where teams of Mexicans came every weekday to mow and edge the lawns. She left the wipers on, but the street remained blurry as tears filled her eyes with sorrow and mystery and loneliness.

That's how she would remember them, like something out of a B-movie, but the image was too indelible to shake. Sirena moved a year later to get an MBA at San Jose State. She was reluctant to give up her old address in case Bullitt tried to contact her. She lay awake many nights, hoping for a tap at her window, only to find Bullitt balanced precariously on the third story sill. Like Peter Pan, he would take her hand, and they would fly through the night sky to Never Never Land, where the other star children lived. It would turn out that each of them could go back for one regular person they truly missed, and Bullitt had come back for her. Devi would be there, her laughter the first thing Sirena would hear upon her arrival, and they would embrace and be like sisters again, the sister neither had before they met.

Never Never Land was Tuva, at least as Sirena imagined it, a country of huge deserts and steep mountains and hard white light. The star children spent their days training and planning how to save each of their worlds, and Sirena and the other regular people would support and encourage them, and just their presence would make the star children glad. Bullitt would wrap his arms around her at night while Devi went off with some other handsome star child, and Bullitt would whisper outrageous stories to her. But now she would believe every word he said, every word that fell from his lips into her ear, whether or not she understood the turning of the universe like a prayer wheel in the palm of his hand.

When Sirena finally got out of the car and went to the door, a young woman partially opened it and looked at her questioningly.

"I'm a friend of Devi's," Sirena said.

The girl opened the door just wide enough to let Sirena slip inside, where she found a room full of women, all Indian, crowded around Devi's mother. She lay in a large chair placed in the middle of the room sprawled in grief. On seeing Sirena, she started to get up, and Sirena opened her arms to hug her, as she had so often before. But Mrs. Parekh began to scream at Sirena in Gujerati, then said, in English, "It was your friend who did this! Who killed her and ran away!"

Devi's father came in from another room and tried to calm her. But she kept screaming a phrase Sirena could not understand even as she was led away, and the other women, even the cousin who had called, stood silently and stared at Sirena. Devi's little brothers were not in sight, and Sirena felt that she did not belong here.

She turned and went out into the rain and got in her car. She was shaking and crying, unsure what to do next or even where to go.

After awhile, Mr. Parekh came out and tapped on her window. Sirena rolled it down.

"I'm sorry," he said. "She is out of her mind with grief. She did not mean what she said."

"I'm sorry, too," said Sirena. "I wish I knew what happened, but I don't. I didn't even know they knew each other."

The rain soaked Mr. Parekh's clothes, but he seemed not to notice. He was a handsome man growing a little fat, but his face was gaunt with fatigue and sorrow.

"I will call later," said Sirena, "you are getting soaked." She reached for her keys.

"Please," he said, leaning in the window to look her in the eye. "Wait until we call you, after she has calmed down, when this has passed a little."

Sirena hesitated. "Will there be a memorial service?"

He hesitated. "It will be family only," he said. "That is our custom."

It was not family only, rather hundreds came, from the Indian community and Devi's workplace and many friends, but Sirena was never called. She read about it in the paper.

Bullitt's parents, too, were suspicious when she called, certain that she knew more than she was telling. But they invited her over for what would be a last time, Sirena could tell, unless there were further developments.

"Bullitt was adopted," said his father, glancing at the smiling face in one of the photos decorating their living room. "Did he tell you that?"

"No!" said Sirena, startled. "He said he was an only child." She started to talk about the scar and the bullet, but it suddenly sounded weird.

"He is an only child," his father said, impatiently, then more softly. "Was. An only adopted child."

"From Tuva? Or here?"

"From here."

His mother sat quietly, making something out of lace. She had barely risen to greet Sirena and serve her tea before sitting down again in silence.

"We were told his mother died at his birth, a bad delivery, a C-section. You know C-section?"

Sirena nodded.

"A single mother," Alex went on. "No father. He has a scar from it, from the delivery."

Sirena swallowed the scalding hot tea Mrs. Tagrib had served her in a glass, burning her throat. The clock ticked loudly.

"I always thought he was from Tuva," said Sirena lamely.

"No. American born." Alex opened the front door and stepped onto the porch and lit a cigarette. He left the door open, raising his chin to blow smoke above his head. "We could not have children of our own,"

Sirena glanced at Mrs. Tagrib, who gazed steadfastly at her handiwork. She seemed to be embroidering Cyrillic letters onto a band of white lace.

"I really need to go," said Sirena, standing. "Thank you for the tea." She set her glass on a side table.

"You have not finished it," said Alex, no warmth in this voice.

"I'm sorry," said Sirena. She had been saying that for days now—to Devi's parents, to her employer, now to Bullitt's parents. "I need to see my grandmother today."

On the sidewalk she turned to Alex, still on the porch smoking. "But if you hear anything ..."

"He is dead," said Alex. "We will have a memorial service. He would not have left that girl in the car."

"No," said Sirena. "That's what I kept telling the police."

She turned and went to her car. Alex finished his cigarette and went back inside, shutting the door as Sirena started the engine. They seemed to blame her, too.

Later, crumpled on the floor at her grandmother's feet, Sirena wrapped her arms around the old lady's knees and cried into the hem of her apron.

Abuela stroked her hair and made clucking, shooshing noises. Then she began to sing an old melody that Sirena remembered from before, when Sirena had been about fourteen.

Sirena had been lying on the couch with a fashion magazine while her grandmother cleaned around her. Sirena had asked what the words, which were in Spanish, meant. Unable to explain, Abuela had gotten out the 1950s English/Spanish dictionary that was kept under the television buried under old newspapers and magazines.

It turned out the song was a hymn from the odd church her grandmother had belonged to and raised Sirena's father in before he married her mother. It had no crosses on the walls and no priests. The song was about the comforts of the afterlife.

"I miss them so much," Sirena said. "It's not fair."

"Están con Dios," said Abuela. They are with God. "In Gehenna."

"What's that?"

"A place where people go after they die."

"Like Heaven?"

"Yes," she said, but with hesitation in her voice.

"Like Purgatory?"

"Yes."

"Do you think they are suffering?"

"No, mija," she said, stroking Sirena's hair. "They have already suffered in life. The song says 'Sinners find rest in Gehenna.' Now they are resting."

To Sirena, Gehenna was like Tuva. It was high and bright and wide with views from the Baltic Sea to China. She could hear singing and bells in the clear air and see children riding horses to school down unpaved streets.

They all looked like Bullitt. They were all waiting for her, but Sirena knew that she would not go there for a long, long time.

Tiny Town

It didn't really bother her until she boarded the little train.

When Sirena was small, her family had sometimes visited the Forresters, and she hadn't noticed anything unusual about their house. Well, yes, there was one thing. The dining room was dominated by a huge wooden cabinet that held glasses, mugs, and "spirits." At first, she hadn't understood the pun, that spirits could be ghosts or alcoholic drinks. Since her parents didn't drink, she had never heard of the other kind of spirits. The cabinet held glasses and mugs shaped like human skulls, and across the top, in huge letters, was carved "Pick Your Poison." She had stared and stared at it until her mother, embarrassed by the whole thing, had asked her to stop.

The Forresters were little people. That is, they were both under five feet tall. She couldn't remember how her family came to know them. There were all these connections that had happened before she was born, and it was difficult for her to imagine all the life that had been led before her own life had begun. It might have had something to do with the Optimists' Boys Ranch, where her father had once worked. Maybe Mr. Forrester was an Optimist. That would make sense. He was certainly cheerful all the time. His nickname was Chick.

Anyway, the Forresters had built the house to suit their size. The downstairs was normal in proportion, but the upstairs was scaled down to accommodate them. It had low ceilings, low counters, and the shower head was positioned about a foot lower on the wall than in a standard home. Sirena did not know about the shower until she had to stay there as a guest after her mother had married Chick Forrester. But that was many years later.

Another thing she remembered about one of those early visits were the Chihuahua dogs. The Forresters never had children, but they kept two dogs that they treated almost like babies. Like all Chihuahuas, they were mean and suspicious of strangers, barking and barking when anyone came to visit. They had been locked in the bathroom when Sirena came over with her mother, but Mrs. Forrester, to distract Sirena from the liquor cabinet, had brought one of them out to show her. Despite all the noise it had been making, the dog was tiny enough to fit in Mrs. Forrester's cupped hands.

"It's called a Teacup Chihuahua," Mrs. Forrester had said, and Sirena wondered out loud if it would really fit in a teacup.

"Oh, it's just an expression," said Mrs. Forrester, "a term they use for really small dogs. There are also teacup poodles, bred especially for their size."

It lay there trembling, and Sirena was afraid to touch it. She decided it was the ugliest thing she had ever seen, uglier than an earthworm. But even at the age of seven, she knew better than to say that.

Some years later, Mrs. Forrester died of a heart attack. Sirena understood that it was not totally unexpected, that she had some heart defect having to do with her size, and Mr. Forrester lived alone for many years, sometimes coming over for dinner. He loved steak and baked potatoes and often complimented Sirena's mother on her cooking. He even liked spicy Mexican food, and Sirena sensed a certain competition between Mr. Forrester and her father over who could eat it the hottest.

Sirena's father liked to tell the story of how he had once eaten food from India at the International Club when he was in college, and it was so hot that someone else had to run from the table and spit out the food in the bathroom. Mostly, she felt that he liked to tell the story so that people would know he had been in the International Club in college. That was about a million years ago, and Sirena and her brother, Danny, used to roll their eyes at each other everytime he told the story. Again, only many years later, did Sirena come to appreciate that Redlands College was considered progressive for its time for admitting people from India and China, even Mexicans who lived just up the arroyo from town like her father. But he was special. Through some miracle, they had waived tuition for him and given him a chance to go to college. If not, the family would all be picking fruit someplace. Not, Sirena thought, her idea of a good time.

After Sirena had grown up and moved away, her father's heart had stopped one day. He had been working in his garden on an especially hot afternoon, and her mother had just come out a few minutes earlier and urged him to come inside.

"I just want to finish watering these trees," he had said. He kept a beautiful garden of vegetables and fruit trees, always fantasizing about being totally self-sufficient if there were some sort of emergency. Sirena wasn't sure what. An earthquake, maybe, since that was the only state of emergency that occurred on a regular basis in San Bernardino. Except for gang fights, and Sirena didn't know how growing your own vegetables was going to help during a gang fight.

Anyway, her mother had looked out the back window and seen her father staggering toward the house, saying something she couldn't understand. She had run outside as he collapsed, then back in the house to call 911. The paramedics put him in the ambulance and took him to St. Bernardine's, but by then it was too late.

It happened the day before Sirena and her husband were planning to leave for Paris, an anniversary trip. Her mother had urged her to go anyway, but Sirena knew she couldn't. They had postponed their trip, getting all but about five hundred dollars back, and she had flown to Ontario and rented a car to go to the funeral. She stayed and helped for about a week, but her mother seemed okay. Danny still lived in the area at the time, and he knew more about finances than she did, so he helped her mother with the funeral arrangements and all the paperwork that goes with a death.

While she was there, Sirena took the opportunity to clean the house, something her mother never thought much about, and carefully packed away her father's worn clothes. She couldn't believe the state they were in; they almost broke her heart. Most of the pants and shirts weren't even fit to give away, but she figured that the Goodwill could resell them for rags. At the same time, her father had carefully preserved the suit he had worn for his high school graduation, a jacket with two pairs of pants that he couldn't possibly have worn again. The habits of a childhood of poverty had never left him. The only newer things were those she had given him over the years. Her brother gave him stuff like travel videos, which he liked a lot.

Sirena and her husband had postponed their trip to Paris for a year, choosing to go with the same tour group, only the following fall. It was wonderful, and Sirena dreamed of saving up enough money to go again.

In the meantime, Mr. "Please, call me Chick" Forrester had continued to go over for dinner. Eventually, he persuaded Sirena's mother to go out for dinner once in a while, so he could treat her. Sirena's mother was tall for a Mexican, 5′8″, and very self-conscious about her height. This was difficult for Sirena to understand, since she was not that tall. But in the 1940's in San Antonio, Texas, this was considered very tall. Her mother never wore heels over one inch and had already tended to stoop when she was out in public with Sirena's father. He always claimed to be 5′8″ as well, but by the time Sirena was a grown-up, she could look over the top of his head. Maybe he had shrunk, she couldn't tell.

Eventually, Chick asked Sirena's mother to marry him. Sirena saw this coming, but Danny did not. Still, they were both surprised that she accepted.

"She must be really lonely," said Sirena.

Danny didn't seem to mind. "If it makes her happy, great," he had said. He and his wife had already moved to the Midwest by then, where she taught at a state college and he was an industrial designer for an upscale bathroom fixtures company. "I'm just glad she has someone to look after her."

The wedding took place while Sirena was in Paris, a year after her father died. It wasn't exactly an elopement, but it was a small ceremony with only a couple of witnesses. Danny was there but wasn't long on descriptive abilities. "It was fine," he said on the telephone. "Short and to the point." They both giggled a little.

The couple honeymooned at the Hotel Coronado in San Diego.

They sold the house in San Bernardino, and their mom moved into Chick's house in Yucaipa. It was a much nicer area, and Sirena and Danny were relieved to get their mother out of the old house. In spite of the neighborhood, which hadn't gotten any better and maybe a little worse over the years, the property sold for almost a hundred thousand dollars, so their mother was doing very well. She even gave some of the money to Danny and Sirena, for which they were grateful, and Chick did not seem to mind.

After that, when Sirena came to visit, she stayed in one of the two upstairs bedrooms. In deference to her mother's height, she and Chick used the one downstairs bedroom, the former guest room. The first time they came to stay, Sirena and her husband banged their heads on everything, and after that, he always found an excuse not to come along. She didn't really blame him. Washing her hair in the shower was something of a trick, and her husband was six feet tall.

"What happened to that thing in the dining room?" asked Sirena on that first visit. The room looked huge without it. In its place stood a small table with artificial flowers in a vase.

"You mean, the spirit cabinet?" asked her mother.

She couldn't even bring herself to say the word "liquor," Sirena thought. "Yes."

Her mother gave a short, embarrassed laugh. "That was the first thing to go."

Chick was retired from the state and had a comfortable pension. He drove a big car that was customized so that he could see over the steering wheel and reach the pedals. He loved to drive, and they often took day trips out into the desert or to drive along the coast, stopping for fancy meals along the way. For Sirena's mother, after thirty years of being married to someone who would only take her out for birthdays and anniversaries, this was the biggest luxury, something she could relate to.

They always went out to eat at least once when Sirena visited. Her mother still got that look on her face, Sirena noticed, when they walked into a restaurant and people stared at them. But with her mother, it would always be something she was embarrassed about—her clothes or her children's manners or some other imagined deficiency. It might as well be Chick, thought Sirena, who swaggered in and acted like he was in charge. In spite of his size and his squeaky voice, people treated him with respect. And he tipped well, too. Sirena got used to the looks, the attention, and the whispering. She even came to enjoy it a little bit since she didn't have to put up with it all the time.

When Chick died, Sirena didn't go to the funeral. She had just given birth to her second child and did not really want to travel. Again, Danny flew out and took care of the details, but it turned out that Chick had everything pre-arranged. He had paid in advance and owned a plot through a sort of cooperative organization.

Danny called Sirena after the funeral. "You won't believe this," he said.

"What?" asked Sirena. She was bored and tired, already, of being home with her new baby. She needed news.

"Chick was buried next to his first wife, but there's room for mom on the other side."

"Well, is that unusual?" she asked.

"I don't think so, except that it's in this place, in Tiny Town."

"Tiny Town? Oh, no." Sirena switched the baby to her other arm so she could hold the phone more easily.

"Well, it's not really called Tiny Town, but that's what I'm calling it. It's called Pleasant Meadows, and it's a section of the Rosemead Memorial Cemetery."

"It's a special place for special people?" guessed Sirena.

"Bingo. And it's all set up for little visitors. It has a train to take people around, so they don't have to get tired walking to the graves."

Sirena tried to imagine this. "It sounds like Disneyland."

"There are a lot of famous people there," said Danny. "Probably a lot of former Disney employees."

"Is mom okay?" asked Sirena.

"Yeah, I think so," said Danny. "She seems sad, sadder than when Dad died."

"Well, who wants to outlive two husbands?"
"That's what she said."

Each of them suspected that she might have done it on purpose, but they never talked about it. Their mother had always been a nervous driver and never took the freeway. After fifty years of living in California, she knew the back way to everywhere, through places her children never even knew existed. That's why, when she wrecked Chick's big Cadillac on Cajon Pass, they both wondered where she was going.

"She wasn't wearing a seatbelt," said Danny, when he picked Sirena up at the airport.

"She hated seatbelts," said Sirena, "but Chick always made her put it on. She didn't still have those big blocks on the pedals, did she?"

"No, I took them off after Chick died."

The road had been icy that morning, and the Highway Patrol put it down as an accident. Afraid that the insurance company wouldn't pay if it was a suicide, Sirena and her brother said nothing about their suspicions. After all, they didn't really know. Their mother got confused sometimes and might have gotten on the freeway by mistake. There was a service at their mother's old church, the one where she had played the piano years before, and a few of her old friends came. She hadn't seen much of them since her re-marriage.

At the cemetery they were greeted by a small person wearing a name tag that said "Rita." She was meticulously dressed in a navy blue suit with a pink blouse. She was so small that it seemed odd for her to be wearing makeup. Sirena decided that Rita must have had all her clothes custom made.

Rita looked up at them in surprise. "Are you …" she looked at a paper she was holding "… Mr. And Mrs. Forrester's children?"

Danny understood her question. "We are Mrs. Forrester's children, the second Mrs. Forrester."

Rita looked at her papers some more. "Oh, I see," she said finally. She led them out of the back of the building, where they boarded the little train. It was tastefully painted in black with white and grey trim, not the gaudy red and yellow that Sirena had imagined. The knee space was so narrow that both Sirena and her brother had to turn sideways to sit down. Rita got in front.

"We'll leave in just a minute," she said. A few other people came out and got on different cars. "Go ahead," said Rita into a sort of walky talky, and the train began to move. At first, it went slowly, then it picked up a little speed.

Danny's family had stayed in Wisconsin, and Sirena's husband was at the house in Yucaipa with their two small children. They intended to stay awhile and put things in order. She thought of them now.

"Sam and Rachel would have enjoyed this," she said.

Rita took this as a cue to be less serious. "It makes it pleasant for the children to come and visit their grandparents," she said.

"Good idea," said Danny.

Sirena was afraid to make eye contact with her brother, afraid one of them would say something that might be offensive to Rita, so she looked out at the trees and small buildings as they passed. Those must be mausoleums, she thought. So many dead people. At regular intervals they crossed pastel-colored walkways that led away from the train tracks. Sirena understood that different parts of the cemetery were color coded. Twice, the train slowed and stopped to let off passengers. Sirena couldn't believe she was riding a toy train to her mother's grave.

At last they arrived at a walkway of yellow brick.

Of course, thought Sirena. It was Pleasant Meadows, the area where their mother would be buried next to Chick. The white and gold coffin, along with two laborers already sweating in the hot sun, was waiting for them. They walked around and looked at Chick's headstone and the earlier one for the first Mrs. Forrester. There was a lttle oval photo of each set into the stone. Mrs. Forrester held one of her beloved Chihuahuas in the photo. Sirena found herself staring at a tiny photo of a tiny woman holding a tiny dog. She suddenly wondered where the dogs were buried.

"Will our mother's headstone have a photo?" she asked.

"If you like," said Rita.

Sirena just nodded. She and Danny would talk about it later. It was just too weird right now. Was it just her imagination, or were the graves closer together, shorter?

They had decided not to have another service at the graveside, but Danny and Sirena both said a few words.

"May she rest in peace," said Danny, and tossed in a carnation that Rita handed to him.

"May they be happy always," said Sirena, and threw in hers. It bounced and went down the side of the coffin, instead of staying on top.

Rita nodded to the laborers to go ahead and fill in the grave, and Danny handed each of them a ten dollar bill. Chick would have liked that, thought Sirena.

They were silent on the train ride back.

At the main building Rita had Danny fill out some forms. He tried to include Sirena, but she couldn't concentrate. She felt numb.

"Do whatever you think is best," she said, "I trust your judgment." After years of working in design, Danny always knew the line between tasteful and too much. Sirena had pretty good taste, too, but right here, right now, Sirena wasn't too sure about anything. She looked at photos on the walls of sample headstones, a brochure for "urn interment."

She heard Rita make a pitch for them to buy plots in the same cemetery.

"It's not normally open to non-members," she heard her say, "but since you are family, it's permissible."

Danny, to Sirena's relief, declined.

Only in the car on the way back to Yucaipa did Sirena suddenly panic. "What about Dad?" she asked.

"What about him?"

"He's all alone in the other cemetery."

"That's okay," said Danny. "What do you want to do, move him?"

"To—Tiny Town?" Sirena dared to look at her brother for the first time.

She watched a little smile form on his face. "Yeah, you heard the lady. There's room for more."

Sirena laughed. "I don't think he would be happy there," she said. And then she started to cry. She hadn't cried until now, and Danny looked around the rental car in vain for Kleenex.

Sirena fumbled in her purse and brought some out, dabbing her nose and eyes. "He always hated being short."

Danny patted her clumsily on the knee, trying to drive at the same time.

"Come on," he said. "I'll take you to Denny's. I'll even let you pick your poison."

"Stop," said Sirena, "I can't take anymore." Now she was laughing and crying.

The car veered back and forth across the lane as Danny tried to watch her and watch the freeway at the same time. "Are you okay?" he asked.

"Yes," she said. "I mean, no." She calmed down enough to blow her nose. "I don't think I ever want to visit Tiny Town again."

"Don't worry about it right now," said Danny. "There's plenty of time to get used to it."

"That's what I'm afraid of," said Sirena. "All the time that stretches ahead." She looked at Danny. "We're the grown-ups now."

Something Even You Can Understand

When they returned home that evening, the cat was outside. She hissed and bolted from the porch at their approach, not the least bit interested in going inside, where they had left her. The play they had seen had been by e.e. cummings, enacted entirely upon a stage floor slanted surreally toward the audience. Sirena was excited and tired at the same time by so many words that were so difficult to understand.

"Here, Frida," she said, worried at the cat's behavior, even though she was, as a rule, anti-social. But Frida would have none of it.

The front door swung open onto a nearly empty living room. The newly purchased carpets were gone, the footstool turned over. The remaining furniture huddled in a corner like dejected sheep, a long scrape across the floor where the rocking chair had been dragged. Most noticeably, the gramophone with its oak horn was missing. They had been robbed. Only the good stuff had been taken, not the out-of-date stereo or the watercolors on the walls Sirena had painted in college. And yes, Sirena's wallet, which she had left in her purse hanging from the coatrack, was missing as well.

A month earlier, someone had worked a long time to carefully remove the new radio and speakers from their ancient Volvo. When they had gone outside the next day, the windows on the car had been all steamed up. They had now been in town three months, slowly trying to adapt to the new-found prosperity that came with John's job. Welcome to Seattle.

Wary at disturbing the burglar, Sirena and John stalked carefully through the house, discovering the window that had been forced up, the backdoor that stood wide open to the chill night air.

The police came a little while later.

"There have been several burglaries like this in your neighborhood," said the officer. "A woman hires a few teenagers to take antiques and carpets. She pulls a van into the alley, loads up, fences it in Vancouver. The kids get to keep the cash and jewelry. They were probably in and out of here in ten minutes."

"Do you know who she is?"

"We have a pretty good idea," he said, but didn't elaborate.

The policeman took down the information in a perfunctory manner. Something about his attitude made it clear that they should not expect to see their belongings anytime soon.

"Make a list of what was taken," he said. "It will probably take you a couple of days to get it sorted out." He placed a call before he left, looked briefly animated before hanging up.

"Your wallet's been found," he said, "at a local grocery store. Someone found it on the sidewalk and turned it in. I'll be right back."

While he was gone, John and Sirena ventured upstairs. Some of her jewelry was missing in a haphazard sort of way—no attention paid to what might be more valuable. None of it was worth much, anyway, but it stung to have someone rifling through her stuff. She took off her dress and put on jeans before the officer returned. By now both she and John were tired and buzzed at the same time—the rush of adrenaline at the danger they had eluded.

The policeman returned with Sirena's wallet. The cash was missing, but her one credit card remained. Oddly, her driver's license was gone as well.

"Definitely kids," said the policeman. "They'll use it for a fake ID."

The return of the credit card was a source of great relief. They had already envisioned bills coming in from car dealers and hotels and stereo stores. Numerous letters and phone calls. Having to re-establish credit.

"At least we were gone when they came," said Sirena. "What if we had been here? What if they were armed?"

"They probably watched the house," said John. "They knew when we were gone."

"But why us?" asked Sirena. "We don't have much. Now we don't have anything worth stealing."

And it was true. The more she thought about that over the next few days as they compiled their list for the police and the insurance company, the more of a comfort it became. Relieved of their beautiful new carpets, carpets they had spent almost two hours picking out at a downtown store, their footsteps echoed on the wood floors. The house, which had just begun to lose its new-house feel, returned to a sort of zen aestheticism stripped down to its essentials.

Upon looking it up in Kovacs's, they discovered that the gramophone was the single most valuable thing they had owned.

"That's probably what made them break in," said John. "You could see the gramophone from the front window."

"You could see the carpets, too," said Sirena.

"Yeah, but it was the gramophone that made them think we might have more worth stealing."

The following Saturday Sirena drank tea in the open front room while the cat lay in a patch of sunlight. The clean oak floors looked enormous without carpets. John spent the day drilling and filing until he had installed deadbolts on the front and back doors. When he was done, it took two keys to get into the house. He hammered metal stops into the ground floor window frames to keep the double-hung windows from being opened more than a few inches.

"There," he said, surveying his work with satisfaction. "Now they'll have to break a window to get in."

They debated the merits of an electronic security system, and John began to gather brochures on them which he studied in the evenings as though cramming for a test.

At night Sirena wondered if someone was watching the house. Maybe there was a bulletin board for burglars, one that said which houses had been hit recently, so that others wouldn't bother. She thought about the girl who must be using her ID, wondered if she was getting drunk or shoplifting things. Bouncers at the clubs would come to recognize her, bar her at the door: "Yeah, that Sirena chick is really wild. Started a fight here last weekend. Don't let her in, or her friends either."

After two weeks they called the police to see if there had been any progress.

No, they were told, but there had been another robbery just like theirs about a block away. Carpets and antiques. The ring was still operating. Chances are, they said, that your stuff is long gone, somewhere in Canada.

"I'll bet they didn't even look for it," said John. He felt bad about the gramophone. It had belonged to his grandmother. The burglars had left the small, heavy records, the carefully preserved manual, and the extra needles behind. Sirena had liked to listen to a recording of a man imitating birds, especially "night sounds of the Okefenokee swamp."

"It would be worth a lot more with the accessories," said John. Like his grandmother, who had been a librarian, John kept everything. Stealing the gramophone without the records didn't make any sense to him, like stealing a car without the tires. He was still recovering from losing his car radio.

They had returned once to look at carpets in the downtown store after the check came from the insurance company but hadn't seen any they liked. The ones they had originally purchased, it turned out, had been unusual, in darker colors with animal designs. Already, Sirena missed the roaming deer, the fanciful creatures that had populated the borders of the carpets. She was not ready to welcome another set of carpets into her front room. Standing in the showroom, too hot in her winter coat, Sirena felt that she was about to cry.

"Do you understand?" she said to John when the impatient salesman was distracted by another customer who was ready to buy.

"Sure," he said. "I'm in no hurry."

One small carpet had been left behind; a wool rug that had been in front of the window forced open with the neighbor's shovel. Sirena would have put it in the front room just to break up the space, but a great, dark, greasy boot print marred the tan surface.

"Maybe we could trace them with this boot print," said Sirena, jokingly. "Match it to another burglary."

They sent it to be cleaned, but the dark mark remained. The stain lingered long after the event, a constant reminder, thought Sirena, that, to others, your home is just another house.

She dreamed one night of the other Sirena, the girl who must be using her driver's license. She dreamed that this Sirena, a teenaged girl, walked into the house one night, just opened the door, and walked in. She came upstairs to where Sirena and John lay sleeping fretfully in their bed, unable to wake up. The other Sirena wore the gold earrings that had been taken in the burglary, the one's from Mexico City with the tiny jade stones. On her hands she wore many rings, rings from other burglaries. She opened the closet and took out some of Sirena's clothes, held them up and admired herself in the mirror on the inside of the door. Then she took off her own jacket and put on some of Sirena's things before leaving.

When Sirena got up the next morning, she opened the closet door, fully expecting to find a strange jacket crumpled there. But nothing was missing, nothing new was in its place—only the sleepy, puzzled look on her own face in the mirror as she stood in her nightgown, tugging at her earlobe, as though trying to remember something she had forgotten.

The next day Sirena got home from work and cleaned out her closet. Out with the flowered dresses, the red cardigan with gold trim on the front. She left a few black skirts and jackets for work, her white shirts, and her jeans. Everything else filled bags and bags. She had always liked clothes.

"What's all this?" asked John when he came in and stepped across the grocery sacks in the hallway. "Are we moving again?"

"No," said Sirena. "I'm just getting rid of a few things. Things that I'll never wear in Seattle."

Every night before he went to bed, John checked all the locks and deadbolts. He checked to see that the windows on the ground floor were secure. He locked the garage from inside, then the fire door between the garage and the basement. At the top of the basement stairs, he locked the door to the kitchen.

"What if there's a fire," asked Sirena, "and I'm in the middle of doing laundry?"

"If you're in the basement, you'll have this door unlatched. Besides, you can always go out through the garage."

"What if I've just come home and you've gone out the front door, leaving the basement door locked and the car catches on fire in the garage?"

"Then you can close the fire door and call the fire department."

"What if the cat is in the garage?"

John looked at her. "Believe me, if the car catches on fire, the cat will not stay in the garage."

Sirena left the house before John in the morning to beat the traffic to the Eastside. After the second time that she left the door unlocked behind her, John asked if this was going to become a habit.

"Well, you're still here," she said. "What's the big deal?"

"What if they come back?"

"The burglars? At seven o'clock in the morning? For what?"

"There are prowlers at all hours looking for unlocked doors."

Sirena looked at him. He was serious. "John," she said, "if it makes you feel better, I will lock the door."

"Good," he said.

"You've changed," said Sirena.

"So have you," said John. "You always wear black."

It was true. Sirena had even started painting her nails black. She had always worn bright colors before, assuming they flattered her honey-colored skin.

She shrugged. "It's different here. The light is different."

‡‡‡

One day, instead of going straight home from work, Sirena stopped at a neighborhood place that served beer and burgers. She ordered a glass of wine and sat staring idly at the heavy traffic on Lake City Way. It was always rush hour in Seattle.

"Sirena!" called the man behind the bar, and she jerked her head around. But he was talking to someone else. A girl came from the other end of the room, where she had been setting up for the dinner crowd. She looked too young to work in a tavern. Unless, of course, she had a fake ID to get the job. Sirena's hands began to tingle.

She looked at her glass, then stared at the girl when she passed nearby. What was she looking for? To see if they looked alike? She found herself looking at the girl's hands and wrists, looking for her own jewelry. The girl had an intensely bored look on her face. She had dark hair like Sirena's but wore a stud in her nostril. Definitely younger.

"How come you're home so late these days?" asked John when Sirena let herself into the house.

"We're on a deadline," she said. It was true, but she had still been going to the tavern after work. It seemed a stupid thing to say to John, I'm watching a girl who might be me.

She always paid cash. Sirena didn't want to have whoever waited on her say, "Hey, we have a Sirena here spelled the same way." The girl herself sometimes came to her table. She seemed unremarkable in every way, this other self, but Sirena eventually heard her mention a club to some people where she and her friends liked to go.

One night when John was out of town Sirena found herself getting in her car and driving downtown. On First Avenue she spotted the place and looked for parking. It took awhile, and when she emerged from her car a couple of blocks away, Sirena put on the glasses she normally used just for working on her computer. I have a right to be here, she kept telling herself. So what if she recognizes me?

Sirena stayed until closing, accepting cigarettes from young people with shaved heads—she couldn't tell if they were boys or girls—oddly soothed by the trance or house music, whatever it was called. The electronic nature of it, the samples of things strangely familiar yet not—put her in a state of revery that she left only reluctantly. Sirena forgot to look for the girl and her friends, did not know if she would have recognized her. She could not remember the last time she had closed a place down.

Back at her car, Sirena could not find her keys. She began to panic, but everything else was in her purse—wallet, cell phone, datebook. She pressed her face against the window to see if her keys were inside. There they were—sitting in plain view on the car seat. She must have set them down to take out her glasses, locking the doors with the button. As she stood there, a cab cruised by, and Sirena hailed it to take her home. She was suddenly too tired to deal with the car. She would get it in the morning. Sirena dreaded trying to explain this to John, who viewed every mistake, every slip in security, as a personal affront. Maybe she just wouldn't tell him, she thought.

At the house Sirena realized that she had no way to get in, but she had the cab drop her off anyway.

Sirena walked between the houses to the alley, then wandered down to the end. She had a vague plan, something that had occurred to her during the nights since the burglary. In the light of the street lamps, everything looked transformed, comforting in an otherworldly sort of way, with the neighbors sleeping all around her. Sure enough, at the end of the block, Sylvia, the unofficial mayor of the neighborhood, had left a ladder leaning against the side of her garage. Lifting it and staggering a little, trying to keep her purse from sliding off her shoulder, Sirena carried it back to her house and placed it against the back wall. She climbed on the roof and pushed up the window she had left unlocked during the heat of the day.

Triumphantly, she climbed in, went downstairs, and returned the ladder to the neighbor. She would have to tell Sylvia not to leave her ladder out from now on.

Sirena went home and climbed the stairs, removing her now filthy clothes as she went. Entering the bedroom, she was shocked to see a form in the bed. She froze at the door, then looked carefully at the still figure. It was John.

He must have come back early, she thought. He could have let her in all along. He looked so peaceful lying there, so vulnerable, the side of his face pressed trustingly into his pillow. She had climbed in the window at the end of the hall making all sorts of noise, and he had slept through it. He must be really tired, she thought. It reminded her of a painting she had seen once, of a man asleep in the desert while a lion watched him. The lion looked benevolent, but the man looked so—alone.

Sirena felt wonder and a sort of elation as she carefully settled into bed. It was almost three o'clock, and she would hate herself when she had to get up in a couple of hours. John would think she was insane when he found out. But for now, Sirena marveled at her discovery, at how easy it was. It was so easy to be somebody else.

About the Author

Kathleen Alcalá is the author of *The Deepest Roots*, a work of speculative nonfiction on sustainability and island living. Her work has received the Governor's Writers Award, the Western States Book Award, and the Pacific Northwest Booksellers Award, among others. A graduate of the MFA Program at the University of New Orleans and the Clarion West Science Fiction and Fantasy Workshop, Kathleen is editing an anthology on La Llorona, the Crying Woman of Mexican mythology, with Norma Elias Cantú. Her novels *Spirits of the Ordinary* and *The Flower in the Skull* have recently been republished by Raven Chronicles Press.

"My books explore forced migrations, identity, and our relationship with the land. Asa descendant of the Jewish expulsion from Spain during the Inquisition, as well as of the Opata Nation of the Sonoran Desert, I have researched and meditated deeply on our ruptured links to the land, and why we choose to honor or degrade it. Speculative writing offers us a way to examine the 'what if's' of climate change, migration, and indigenous futurisms."